SONG *of the* SWORD

PRAISE FOR SONG OF THE SWORD

"This is a fantasy of epic proportions, with the perfect blend of suspense; well-developed, likeable characters; and a touch of sarcastic humour."
—*School Library Journal*

"Every so often . . . a writer is skilled enough to utilize the stories of King Arthur and Camelot to significant effect . . . a taut, compelling narrative, well-drawn characters, and a keen sense of genuine peril and true wonder. It's a powerful, fun, engaging read, and it's the first of a series, so readers have much to look forward to."
—*Quill & Quire*

"Willett's novel will please fantasy junkies with its intricate details; yet there's also an appealing poetry to Ariane's story, best manifested when she learns to use her powers to merge with water and transport herself wherever it flows. *Song of the Sword* is a unique twist on the old subjects of teenage rebellion and self-discovery."
—*Montreal Review of Books*

"One thing that makes this tale different from many in the genre is that it is set in Regina, SK, and full of other Canadian place names, such as Yellowknife and Toronto. The story will appeal to those who enjoy fantasy and will not require a knowledge of the Arthurian tales to follow."
—*CM: Canadian Review of Materials*

"A tight story, and [the] characters exhibit honest emotions . . . Fantasy references galore should ensure that readers who enjoy fantasy—and Arthurian legend in particular—come away satisfied"
    —*Kirkus Reviews*

"The story . . . has wonderful Canadian references and some really funny passages. Ariane is constantly in danger, and the suspense is beautifully maintained."
    —*Helen Wilding Cook*, Library Bound

". . . an exciting plot that gives a great new spin to a favourite story. It can also take credit for a great cast of characters . . . set up to play out what might become the battle of the ages. I can see that exciting adventures await as they all struggle to decide what's worth fighting for: power, friends, or family."
    —*think. thank. thought.*

". . . it was very well done indeed . . . Willett did an excellent job here . . . Ariane [has] quite a bit of personality and spunk."
    —*Word for Teens*

THE SHARDS OF EXCALIBUR
BOOK 1

SONG *of the* SWORD

EDWARD WILLETT

SHADOWPAW
PRESS *Reprise*

SONG OF THE SWORD
The Shards of Excalibur
Book One

Published by
Shadowpaw Press
Regina, Saskatchewan, Canada
www.shadowpawpress.com

Second edition July 2021
First edition published 2014 by Coteau Books

Copyright © 2014 by Edward Willett
All rights reserved

All characters and events in this book are fictitious.
Any resemblance to persons living or dead is coincidental.

No part of this book may be reproduced in any form or by any electronic or
mechanical means, including information storage and retrieval systems,
without written permission from the author, except for the use of brief
quotations in a book review.

Print ISBN: 978-1-989398-14-2
Ebook ISBN: 978-1-989398-09-8

Edited by Matthew Hughes
Cover designed by Tania Craan

Four nieces and a nephew—five books
This one is for Wendi

❧   I   ❧

A WALK IN THE MIST

THE MORNING after she'd been suspended from her new school for fighting, Ariane woke, gasping, from a dream.

It wasn't her first dream of water and swords and knights in armour. But it was the most violent. She stared up into the darkness, for a moment not even sure where she was. She'd slept in a lot of different rooms since her mother had vanished and she'd been placed in foster care. In the dark, they all looked the same.

But then she remembered. She wasn't in foster care anymore. She was living with her Aunt Phyllis, just a few blocks from the house where she used to live with her mother. And unless she got up and got moving, she'd have to tell Aunt Phyllis about her suspension—and she didn't want to do that. Let the school break the news to her. Ariane could explain to her later what had *really* happened . . . if she'd listen.

She'd set the alarm for 6:30, an hour earlier than usual,

but when she glanced at the glowing green numbers, she saw she'd woken up ten minutes before it would go off. The dream that had seemed so vividly real seconds before was already fading, only one image remaining: sun glinting off the blade of an upraised sword.

Over and over, night after night for days now, that same image. Was it from a movie? Not that she could remember. And in real life, she had never even *seen* a sword. So why did she keep dreaming about one?

She sighed and killed the alarm, then rolled out of bed, rubbed her eyes, got up and half-stumbled to the bathroom, where she set the water running while she got out of her pyjamas. She slipped under the spray of hot water, and—

ARIANE STOOD upright in a turquoise lake, the water beneath her supporting her as surely as stone. Though her head was below the surface, she felt no need to breathe. Though the filmy gown she wore billowed around her, it didn't drag her down.

At arm's length over her head she held a sword, the blade in the open air, her hand gripping the hilt just above the surface. Icy rivulets ran down the blade and over her fingers and wrist.

She heard a creak and splash, the sounds distorted by the water: a boat, moving toward her, a lone man pulling at the oars. The rippled surface distorted his face and figure. He stopped rowing. The boat slid closer. He leaned over the gunwale reaching for the sword. His fingers brushed hers as he took the hilt from her, and at his touch—

ARIANE RETURNED TO THE SHOWER, and to the hot water cascading from her shoulders, down her back and legs, so different from the cold water of the lake. Shuddering, she twisted the tap closed, then stood dripping, breathing hard.

It was another dream. It had to be. But she wasn't asleep. She was awake, soaking wet in the shower, staring at the water falling from her hair onto the chrome spout of the bathtub. So it *hadn't* been a dream. It had been . . . what did you call a dream you had while you were awake?

I'm hallucinating, she thought, her heart pounding in her chest. *Seeing things. People who see things are crazy. Does this mean I'm going crazy?*

Like Mom?

No. It was just . . .

She didn't know what it "just" was. But she knew she didn't want it to happen again.

She couldn't bring herself to resume her shower. She dried in a hurry, dressed, pulled on her old leather motorcycle jacket, and headed downstairs. Scary visions or not, she still wanted to be out of the house before Aunt Phyllis woke up.

The hinges on the front door shrieked when she tugged it open. Ariane held her breath and waited to see if the noise had woken her aunt, but she didn't hear anything.

She relaxed, then jumped as something small and black darted through the door and over her feet. "Pendragon!" she said, much louder than she'd intended.

"Mrrrow?" The black cat with the ridiculous name

wound around her ankles, then trotted toward the kitchen and looked back expectantly. "Mrrree?"

"You'll just have to wait until Aunt Phyllis is up!" Ariane whispered. *Which she'll be any minute if I don't get out of here!*

Was that the creak of an upstairs floorboard? Ariane darted into the entryway, pulling the inside door shut behind her. The outside door was unlatched and ajar, which was how Pendragon had managed to get into the front porch and give her an early-morning heart attack. She went out, then turned and gave the door a good hard shove. It closed with a thump, and Ariane heard Aunt Phyllis calling a query. She turned and fled into the pre-dawn twilight, running until she was safely down the street and out of sight of her aunt's bedroom window.

Slowing to a walk, she continued north to College Avenue, then turned west. Crossing Winnipeg Street, she passed St. Dunstan High School to her left—and then, right next door to it, her own new school, Oscana Collegiate. Blood rushed to her cheeks at the memory of the previous day's humiliation.

They'd been waiting for her by her locker. Four girls, older: seniors. She'd known who they were, of course, even after only a week in the school. Shania McHenry. Felicia Knight. And their two hangers-on—nobody ever seemed to bother to remember their names. They were popular. They were ruthless. And they knew exactly how to keep their petty tyranny hidden from the adults who supposedly enforced the rules.

Even if she hadn't known this particular gang, she would

have expected to find one like it at Oscana, because there was one like it—sometimes more than one—in every school. And they always seemed to single out Ariane for special attention. They picked on the weak and the vulnerable. A newly arrived foster brat was their natural prey.

It had started the way it always started. Shania—the pack leader—had blocked her way, sneering. "You're Ariane Forsythe. The *new* girl." She managed to make it sound like an insult.

But Ariane had been through it all before, and she knew the best defense was offense: catch them off-guard, give it right back to them. It was just words, and she was always better at words than *they* were. She raised her eyebrows in mock surprise. "Amazing," she said. "I would've expected you to be too hung over to hear them introduce me over the PA."

But then it went beyond words. They knocked her books out of her hands, and Felicia, number two in the pecking order, stepped on her pencil case and smashed it.

Even then, Ariane held her temper in check. They *don't win if you don't react*, she told herself. *Stay calm*. But then . . .

Shania slammed Ariane's locker shut, the door just missing Ariane's ear. "I heard about you, Airy-Anne," she said in a sing-song voice. "Most kids go into foster homes because their parents can't take care of them. But not you. Your dad ran out on you before you were born. Then your *mom* ran out on you. I hear she went crazy first. You must have done something pretty bad to—"

Ariane lunged, driving Shania across the corridor so hard

her head slammed into the lockers on the far side. A moment later they were rolling on the floor, Ariane fighting in cold silence, Shania screaming obscenities. The others got over their shock and joined in, but then the vice-principal, Mr. Stanton, broke it up. He let the pack go ("Ariane just hit Shania," one of the hangers-on explained, in a voice like an angel, "for no reason at all!") and marched Ariane into the office.

And that had been that. Ariane had been suspended for three days for fighting. Since yesterday had been Thursday, that meant she couldn't go back to school until Wednesday. After that, she'd have supervised detention for a week, one hour after school, in the library, every day. She'd been given a letter that both she and her aunt had to sign before she could return to class. And Mr. Stanton had made it clear he would be phoning her aunt this morning.

Which, of course, was why Ariane was already out of the house, before the sun was even quite up.

She tore her eyes away from the school and refused to look at it again as she strode resolutely down College Avenue. *Yeah, that'll teach it,* she mocked herself. *It's just a building, silly. It's not the cursed castle of some malevolent wizard.*

And the trees lining the sidewalk were just trees, but when she glanced up, their interlocking branches made her think of skeletal hands joining bony fingers.

Too much imagination. How often had she heard that? "You spend too much time in your head, Ariane," Aunt Phyllis would say. "All those books you read, and those weird movies and TV shows. You need to spend more time dealing with the real world. Then maybe you'd do better in school."

Ariane had never believed her. She'd thought the fantasy and science fiction and historical novels and movies and TV shows she devoured were the only things that had kept her sane since her mother had disappeared, while she'd moved from foster home to foster home and from school to school until her Aunt Phyllis had at last recovered enough from her long battle with cancer to rescue her from the system. But after the disturbing vision she'd had in the shower, Ariane wondered if, instead of keeping her sane, those things were doing just the opposite. *Maybe Aunt Phyllis is right. Maybe my imagination is starting to leak into the real world. Why else would I hallucinate holding up a sword out of a lake?*

She crossed Broad Street. Old university buildings made of red brick and Tyndall stone loomed in the mist ahead of her like gothic castles, complete with battlemented towers. *There you go again!* That *building's a movie soundstage now. There's nothing mysterious about it.*

She walked south past the old buildings toward the park surrounding Wascana Lake. The mist thickened as she approached the water, but she didn't mind the cold and damp. In fact, she liked it. She crossed the road that wound through the park and walked down a long, narrow parking lot. At the far end, a few large boulders had been placed on the lakeshore. Beyond them, the pewter-coloured water faded away after only a few metres into a thick blanket of fog just beginning to turn golden as the sun at last climbed above the horizon. She paused to savour the sight. She could be anywhere, in any time. *Anywhere other than Regina,* she thought. A fierce longing to escape the misery her life had been for the past two and a half years welled up in her so strongly it threatened to choke her. *Any time other than now.*

Alas, she knew better. In reality, the lake held nothing but a few small islands. The largest, Willow Island, no more than thirty or forty metres from where she stood, was a popular picnic spot.

She continued to the water's edge, sat down on one of the boulders, and pulled her knees to her chest. Resting her chin on them, she stared into the fog. She loved Aunt Phyllis . . . or at least she knew she was supposed to. And she knew the only reason it had taken her aunt so long to take her in was because of her health problems. She shouldn't resent her for that.

But she did. Her aunt had been in hospital when Ariane's mother, Phyllis's little sister, had disappeared. Ariane had had to deal with all of that herself . . .

Her breath caught in her throat. The vision that leaped unbidden to her mind this time wasn't a hallucination. She wished it were.

She'd been barely thirteen. Her mother, who had only recently begun letting her stay home alone, had said she was going for a walk around the lake and would be back within an hour.

But she wasn't. She wasn't back after two hours, and then three, and then four. Ariane had sat in the living room, in the big armchair by the phone, waiting for it to ring, for her mother to call, or the police, or the hospital—*someone* to tell her what was going on, what to do. In the end she'd fallen asleep.

At 2 a.m. she'd woken up, but not because the phone had rung. Someone was on the front porch, fumbling with the lock. And then there'd been a kind of moan, and a thud.

Terrified, she'd crept into the living room and peered out through the curtains—only to see her mother crumpled on the steps. Ariane had run into the entryway, fumbled open the door, dashed outside in her stocking feet.

Mom's eyes had been open, but not focused. She'd been soaked to the skin, and shivering—it had been early spring, and still dipping below freezing most nights, though the snow had gone. It looked as if she'd hit her head when she'd fallen: there was blood everywhere. Ariane had run back inside and called 911. The ambulance had come, and the police, and there had been questions, and . . .

. . . and just like that, her life had fallen apart. Her mom wasn't making sense, they told her. She kept saying she'd met someone, a strange woman who had pulled her into the lake, but she wouldn't say how or why.

The worst of it was that she wouldn't even *talk* to Ariane. She'd close her eyes whenever Ariane came into the room, yell that she didn't know her, tell the nurse to take her away. She swore Ariane wasn't her daughter, that she didn't *have* a daughter.

A psychotic break, the doctors said. Had there been any warning signs? Had her mother used drugs? So many questions. A neighbour had taken Ariane in. Her mom was going to be kept in the psychiatric ward for a while. And then . . .

then had come the phone call at the neighbour's house. Her mom had vanished. Escaped from the hospital. No sign of her.

And there had been no sign of her ever since.

Ariane squeezed her arms more tightly around her legs. Ever since then, she'd been trying to hold herself together, trying to keep Ariane, the old Ariane, intact. It had never been easy. And now . . . the hallucination in the shower . . .

Am I losing touch with reality too? Did I inherit something—some mental illness—from Mom?

And in that moment of self-doubt, Ariane heard the sound of chanting, coming from the lake.

$\maltese$ 2 $\maltese$

THE STAIRCASE IN THE WATER

Wally Knight jerked awake in the dark and lay still for a moment, heart pounding. The dream . . . the battle . . . the enemy had . . .

But the details were already fading. Which was too bad, because what he could remember of it—clashing steel and blood everywhere—had been awesome.

He looked at his bedside clock, the docked iPhone rising atop it like the monolith from 2001: *A Space Odyssey*, and groaned. It was already 6:20, and he wanted to be out of the house in twenty minutes, just to make sure he didn't bump into his sister Felicia. He'd originally planned to walk to one of the coffee shops on the other side of the lake and hang out there until school, but suddenly he had a better idea.

I'll ride my bike around the lake a couple of times, he thought. *It'll be cool to see the lake as the sun comes up. He grinned in the darkness. I wonder why I never thought of doing it before?*

He was up and dressed and kinda-sorta washed and

combed and out of the house fifteen minutes later, easing his bike out of the garage between his dad's BMW and his mom's Prius, then mounting it and darting across Albert Street into Wascana Park.

He took the first lap of the lake at breakneck speed, revelling in the relative scarcity of joggers on the path and in the cold invigorating kiss of the mist against his cheeks, furiously pedalling away the anger and humiliation left over from the previous night—courtesy, of course, of his sister Felicia.

She'd failed to come home for supper—again; since she'd been hanging out with Shania McHenry and the other members of what Wally privately thought of as "the coven," she'd been coming home later and later—and Ms. Carson, the housekeeper who looked after them while their parents were away, she of the pinched expression and (Wally suspected) never-pinched behind, had blamed *him*.

"You should have told her to come home right after school," Ms. Carson had scolded him. "Honestly, Walter, when are you going to learn a little responsibility?"

Wally had long ago given up trying to argue Ms. Carson out of her passionate belief in his sister's infallibility. *Maybe Flish's little clique really is a coven. Maybe they've put a spell on Ms. Carson.*

On second thought, that couldn't be true, or by now Flish would've turned him into a toad.

With Felicia absent, Ms. Carson wasn't about to waste her time on the pasta dinner she'd originally planned, so Wally had to make do with cold salmon sandwiches and the wilted remnants of the previous night's salad. He retreated to his room as soon as he could, to spend the evening playing the real-time strategy game he'd bought over the weekend.

He usually played first-person shooters and flight simulators, but for some reason the game's medieval setting had appealed to him, and he was beginning to find building castles and mustering armies addictive.

After a couple of hours, he paused to massage his wrist, wrapped in a tensor bandage. He'd sprained it during fencing practice that afternoon. Natasha Mueller, the fencing instructor, had sent him off to the office to get a (highly prized, in Walter's book) get-out-of-gym-free note . . . which was how he'd happened to be in the hallway just in time to see the new girl, Ariane Forsythe, in a knock-down, drag-out fight with Shania McHenry, while Felicia stood nearby looking pleased with herself, and how he'd happened to be in the office when Ariane was suspended for fighting. He'd felt sorry for Ariane. Just at school a week, and already Flish's coven had targeted her for humiliation. He wondered if she'd last out the year.

He resumed playing, but hit the pause key when he heard his bedroom door open. Ms. Carson, for all her faults, always knocked. Which meant—

Whack! The slap on the back of his head almost pushed his nose into his keyboard. He spun his chair to face Felicia. "Hello to you, too. And, for the record—ow!"

Rubbing his stinging scalp, he looked up at his sister. Way up. Felicia was thirty centimetres taller than him even when he was standing. He kept waiting for his fabled adolescent growth spurt in the hope it would even things up, but so far he'd been disappointed. Until it happened, he remained at her mercy when it came to physical confrontation. Which, with Felicia, it always did.

"Where are my books?" she said. "I didn't see them

downstairs."

"I put them in your room."

"You went into my room without permission?"

"Logically, 'take my books home' implied permission to put them in your room—"

"You never go in my room unless I let you in. Which I won't. Got it?"

Wally sighed. "Got it."

"Good." Felicia turned to go.

"So what are you going to do to that new girl?" Wally heard himself say the words, but he obviously hadn't consulted his brain first.

Felicia stopped in the doorway and turned around. "What do you know about it?"

"I saw what happened."

"She attacked Shania. Crazy bitch."

Wally manfully did not ask if those final two words were meant to apply to Shania or the unfortunate new focus of the coven's attentions. "She was in the office when I was getting my excuse-Wally-from-gym note. She looked nice enough. Except for the bruises."

"She's a ratty foster brat, and she's only gotten a *little* of what she's got coming to her. That's all you need to know." Felicia strode across the room and leaned into his face. "Stay away from Ariane Forsythe if you know what's good for you. I don't want my brother hanging out with trash like that."

Wally had memories of a big sister who used to take him to movies and malls and midways, but then he also had memories of parents who took him to the playground, came to his school plays, and put him in his PJs at night. Now his parents were never home, and his sister *wished* she wasn't.

Wally figured the two things were related, but knowing part of the reason Felicia was the way she was didn't change the fact she could—and would—mop the floor with him if he crossed her.

That didn't mean he always had to do what she wanted. It just meant he had to be smart enough not to get caught.

"Got it," he said. "Hadn't you better get going on your homework?"

She shoved his chair so that it had crashed into the computer desk. The computer beeped and rebooted, wiping out a good twenty minutes of game play. Then Felicia had stalked out and slammed the door behind her so hard Wally's LEGO model of the *Millennium Falcon* had fallen from its shelf and exploded across the floor: a good twenty hours' work destroyed, just like that.

Wally, remembering it again, started pumping the bike pedals harder. He zipped down the little hill from the Willow Island overlook to the empty parking lot . . . and then skidded to a halt as the strange sound filling the misty air registered on him. Who would be chanting at this time of the morning—or any time of the morning—out here?

The sound came from the water. He looked that way and saw a girl standing just a few metres away, on one of the boulders on the shore. Even though he couldn't see her face, he recognized her from the day before.

Ariane?

ARIANE GASPED as the chanting rose up from the water, wrapping her in its impossible sound. She'd always loved the cool, solemn cadences of Gregorian chant, but this song held nothing of church or cloister. Wild and untamed, it sounded as if the water itself were singing of rainstorms and creeks and waterfalls and clouds, of all the shapes it had taken, all the places it had been, through its endless, timeless cycle.

She was standing, though she didn't remember getting up from the boulder. The chant wasn't just music: it was a *call*. A call from someone or something that wanted her . . . *needed* her.

Loved her?

And just like that, she thought she knew what—*who*— was calling her. *Mom!* Somehow, impossibly, her mother was in the water, urging her to join her, to reunite with her at last.

Without even thinking about it, Ariane stepped off the boulder and walked into the lake.

She found herself standing on the water, as easily and naturally as if it were the checkered linoleum of her own kitchen floor. The strange music swelled around her, the water exulting that she had answered its call.

A section of the lake in front of her sank and folded like a sheet of silk into a shimmering staircase that led into the depths of the lake.

What *depths of the lake? Wascana Lake doesn't* have *any depths. This can't be happening. It's another hallucination. It has to be.* But her inner voice couldn't reason away the surging waves of welcoming music and the yearning that gripped her, the irrational certainty that if only she listened to that call and walked into the lake, she would at last be reunited with her mother. Her doubts shoved aside, Ariane started down the steps that couldn't possibly exist.

As she did so, the watery music faded into a quiet,

contented hum, like Pendragon purring in a patch of sunlight. Twenty or thirty steps down, she reached a landing. She glanced back at the rectangle of open air through which she had entered, and wondered, just for an instant, what would happen to her if the opening closed. She hesitated, but the water burst into full-throated song, almost anxiously urging her onward. She turned her back on daylight and continued down.

The steps ended in a curtain of falling drops, like a veil of diamond beads. The watery ceiling flickered and quivered above. When Ariane touched the veil, it flowed around her hand. She could feel the cool brush of liquid, but when she drew her fingers back, they weren't even damp.

"Come in, daughter," said a feminine voice from beyond the veil. "Don't be afraid."

That voice . . .! "Mom?" Ariane cried. She pushed through the veil.

She found herself in a flickering, shimmering chamber. Shafts of watery sunlight struck the rippled floor, glancing off it in spikes of diamond light that nearly blinded her. "Mom?" she called again.

"No," answered the voice. "I'm sorry."

A wrenching sob escaped Ariane. She had been so *sure*.

"Come closer," the voice called. The shafts of sunlight coalesced around a raised platform at the far end of the chamber. A woman, tall and regal, clad in a long, flowing dress, watched her from a liquid throne. Behind the woman, a wall of water fell soundlessly into white foam.

Then Ariane felt a chill, as though she had been plunged into a cold pool. The woman was *made of water*. Her hair and dress were only foam, and her arms, fingers, neck and head were as smooth and transparent as polished glass.

"At last," the watery apparition said, and Ariane wondered how she could ever have mistaken that rippling, musical voice for her mother's.

She found her own voice. "Who *are* you?"

The woman spread her glass-like hands. "I am, or was, the Lady of the Lake."

Ariane blinked. "Like in King Arthur?"

"It was I who gave Excalibur to Arthur," the Lady said. "I received it back again when he lay dying at Camlann. I sent Lancelot to Camelot. And I persuaded Viviane to imprison Merlin more than a thousand years ago." She shook her head. "Little did I know how short a millennium truly is."

Ariane stared at the Lady. Everything she said was impossible. Everything that had just happened—that was still happening—was impossible. Ariane was standing in a chamber deep under the water of Wascana Lake—deeper, in fact, than the lake itself!—conversing with a living water-sculpture. It couldn't be happening. None of it.

Her knees gave way and she sat down heavily on the watery floor—the *dry* watery floor, she noted with a tinge of hysteria. She pushed her palms against it. It felt like hard rubber. "I've gone crazy, haven't I?" she whispered. "Just like Mom."

The Lady stepped down from the dais, and knelt beside her. Her transparent hand caressed Ariane's cheek for a moment, and her cool, dry fingers felt as solid as her own. "You are very like your mother, you know," she said softly, and Ariane's head shot up at that. She stared at the vision.

"My mother? You knew—"

"We met," the Lady said. "Two and a half of your years ago, I tried to give her what I now offer to you. She refused."

Ariane blinked. "What . . . what did you try to give her?" And then she felt a surge of anger. Her mother had come home soaking wet, had gone crazy . . . *"What did you do to her?"*

"I did nothing to her," the Lady said sadly. "She would not let me. She refused the power I offered her. Power to save the world."

"Save the world?" Ariane looked about her. "From *what?*"

"Not from what, but from whom," the Lady said. "Merlin." She made the name sound poisonous. "Merlin seeks the shards of Excalibur, scattered around the world. He seeks to re-forge the sword and use its power to seize control, first of this world, then of our world, the world of Faerie. *He must not succeed.* The shards of Excalibur are mine, and must remain mine."

"Then why don't you—"

"I no longer live in this world, and the door between Faerie and Earth is all but closed. I can do very little here now but send dreams and, with great effort, this pale projection of myself. But my heir *can* act in this world. If she accepts the power I can give her, she can defeat Merlin. She can find the shards of Excalibur. She can save your world. And mine."

"Your . . . heir?" Ariane stared at the Lady's glass-like face.

"Your mother, until she rejected my power," the Lady said. "Now, you."

Ariane's heart pounded. "I *have* gone crazy."

"No." The Lady took Ariane's hand in her smooth, cold fingers, and pulled her to her feet. "I am neither a ghost nor a hallucination. I am as real as you." She suddenly turned and stared at the veil behind Ariane, frowning. "As real as . . ." She released Ariane, strode to the veil, and thrust a hand through it. "This *eavesdropper!*"

With a jerk, the Lady pulled into the chamber a boy, younger than Ariane, with unruly red hair and wide green eyes in a face so white every freckle on it stood out as though drawn with a brown felt pen. Ariane had no idea what his name was, but she'd seen him just the day before: he'd been in the office while she was getting suspended. She remembered him staring at her, his eyes almost as wide then as they were now.

Ariane gaped at him. *It's really happening. It's all real.* It couldn't be her imagination, because there was no way she would ever imagine this geeky kid, silently opening and closing his mouth like a landed fish, staring at the Lady as though afraid she might turn him into a frog. *She probably could if she wanted to*, Ariane thought. Certainly the Lady was examining the boy as if she were a biologist and he a particularly peculiar specimen of amphibian. "Astonishing," she murmured. "Of *course* you would be drawn to me. But I didn't know . . . I wonder if Merlin . . ."

But whatever she wondered, she didn't say. The boy suddenly yelped and dug frantically in his pocket, digging out a smartphone that he dropped the moment he had it. "It's hot!" he said, staring down at it. The phone's screen blazed white, and steam rose all around it.

The water-woman stared down at the phone, mouth

open, hand outstretched. For a moment, she looked as frozen and lifeless as the glass statue she resembled. Then a single drop of water formed at the end of her nose and dropped to the floor with a musical "plink." At the sound, the Lady returned to life again. "No!" she cried. "You have revealed me to him!"

Ariane stared at her. "Revealed you to who? What's wrong?"

"Listen!" the Lady said.

Ariane listened, and heard the trickling of water behind her. She turned and saw a thin stream flowing down the watery steps that led up to the sunlit world.

As she watched, that trickle grew.

"I have a bad feeling about this," the geeky kid muttered.

Ariane scrambled to her feet. "We have to get out of here!" she cried.

But the Lady grabbed her wrist, making her yelp, the transparent fingers as solid as steel. "Not yet!" the Lady cried. "You must listen! I have only seconds. Remember: Excalibur will call to you. Follow its song. Find it, all of it, before Merlin does. Your whole world depends on it." The trickle grew to a frothing stream. Water, cold as ice, flowed into Ariane's shoes. "Your mother refused to accept the power. But you must. You must! *There is no one else.*"

She released Ariane's wrist, but then, quick as a striking snake, seized her face in both hands. Ariane gasped. The Lady's palms, at first cool against her cheeks, suddenly blazed with heat. Deep within the water-woman's clear gaze, Ariane saw twin blue pools the colour of midsummer sky. Those pools rushed toward her, then swallowed her whole.

The chamber and the cold water lapping at her ankles

faded from her senses. She felt as though she were floating in a warm lake, fathoms deep. The sound of waterfalls and rushing creeks filled her head and formed strange words: *Gadewch y dyfroedd byw ynoch, a chi o fewn y dyfroedd. Ypˆwer yn eiddo i chi.* Though the language was one she had never heard, Ariane somehow knew what the words meant: "Let the waters live within you, and you within the waters. The power be yours." And indeed, she sensed the power within the strange phrases, so much power that, just for a moment, she felt luminescent, ablaze with light, like a living star, so much so that as she became aware of the chamber again she thought she could see light streaming from her skin, outshining the diluted rays of the sun far above.

But then the Lady thrust her away, and the light disappeared. Instantly Ariane felt the cold embrace of the water again, up to her knees now, pulling and sucking at her calves. Her teeth began to chatter.

"Go!" the Lady cried. Her once-perfect form dripped and sagged. "This place will soon cease to exist! Go! Accept the power! Find the shards of Excalibur! Stop him!" She turned her dripping face toward the boy. "I charge *both* of you with this quest! You must help her!"

"Both of us?" Ariane shot a startled look at the strange red-headed kid, but he was already splashing toward the exit, his malfunctioning phone lost beneath the water. Ariane followed, but she paused at the dissolving archway. She looked back, hoping for a farewell: a final charge or a benediction.

Instead, she saw the figure of the Lady melt away. One moment she was there; the next, a column of water splashed to the floor of the chamber, raising a wave that raced out and lapped around Ariane's waist. Ariane stared, then fled, splashing up the stairs through the descending torrent like a salmon swimming upstream.

MERLIN RAISED his aching head from the surface of the desk and ran a shaking hand through sweat-soaked steel-grey hair. His racing heart began to slow. It had taken all his strength, but he had driven the Lady's consciousness back into Faerie, out of this world—*his* world—once more.

But had it been in time?

Two and a half years ago, the last time she had tried this, had been his moment of greatest peril. He had been weaker then, his thin-stretched web of magic able to sense what was happening but unable to transmit any of his sadly diminished power to put a stop to it. But for whatever reason, the Lady failed to bestow her power on the human woman she had called to herself, her heir in this age. He didn't know why. Nor had he been able to discover who the woman had been, though he had tried.

Now the Lady had made a second attempt. This time a thread of his magic had been close enough that he had not only sensed her presence but had been able to respond swiftly. But had he been swift enough?

And to whom had she attempted to give her power? The same woman, or someone else?

He frowned. If the Lady had succeeded, if some mortal now had the Lady's power, then he faced a potentially dangerous adversary. In Faerie, the Lady had had some skill with water; on Earth, she ruled over water like a goddess.

And though she could never return to Earth in her own body—the door between Earth and Faerie would have to swing wide for that to be possible, and the Faerie Queen and Council of Clades would never permit it—anyone she had given her power to would have far more magic to draw on than he did. His magic came entirely from Faerie, and with the door so nearly shut, he could draw on only a sad trickle of the vast might he had once wielded. But the source of the Lady's power was all the fresh water of the Earth. From Faerie she drew only the ability to use that power.

One day, with Excalibur in his hand, he would *force* that door open from this side, regain his full strength, and march through at the head of a mighty army to unite both worlds under his reign . . . *as should have happened long ago* . . . but until then . . .

Of course, had they been able to, the Queen and Council would have long since closed the portal between the two worlds completely, cutting him off from Faerie, tearing away the last vestiges of his magic, and sentencing him to live, and soon die, as a mortal man. He rubbed the ruby stud he wore in his pierced right ear, and smiled. But they could not close that door completely. He had seen to that. And so he still lived—as did his vision of a united Faerie and Earth.

Few in Faerie now shared that vision, but once, many had.

Not least, the Lady of the Lake.

The thought brought a familiar pang, like the twinge of an old injury. Time had numbed but never fully healed his grief at the loss of the love and friendship they had once shared as brother and sister, he the Lord of Clade Avalon, she his strong right arm. *If only she were still at my side . . . we would be invincible!*

He shook his head, dragging his thoughts out of the distant past. "Would-haves" and "should-have-beens" were a waste of energy. The cold, sword-sharp fact was that the Lady had turned against him, agreeing to carry out the edict of the Queen and Council that he be eternally imprisoned "for the good of Faerie." His lip curled. *For the good of Faerie? For her own ambition!* With him trapped on this side of the portal between the worlds, she must have become sole ruler of Avalon.

But her position could never be completely secure while he still lived and wielded power. And so she had attempted, once again, to raise up a new version of herself to fight him. And once again, she had done so in, of all places, Regina.

He would investigate further. Not in person, of course. Once, magic could have whisked him instantly to the prairie city, no matter how far he would have had to travel. No longer. But no matter. Even in the old days, he had far more often used servants to carry out his designs than done the work himself.

For a moment he toyed with the idea of calling on the demon he had summoned and enslaved long ago, breaking innumerable laws of Faerie in the process, but he rejected the notion at once. Controlling the treacherous creature was exhausting, weakened as he was. *Besides, I may have more need of it later. For now, I think an earthly servant will do.*

He rubbed his aching temples. The Lady might be able to control water, but his skill had always lain with controlling people.

It was a basic principle of magic that everything had a

True Name, a magical name that, if learned and spoken, could be used to command it. In Faerie, those Names were jealously guarded, and to discover a handful had taken him many years. But on Earth . . .!

On Earth, True Names were easily discovered by those who knew where to look, and the limitless power flowing through the open portal from Faerie in those early years had enabled him to make free use of them. In short order, on first arriving on Earth, Merlin had learned the Name of lightning, and how to call it as he willed. He had learned the Names of many birds and animals, so that he could see through their eyes, hear through their ears, and use them as his agents and spies. And he had learned the Names of many, many men and women he could use as pawns in his games of intrigue.

Because he knew the Names of *some* humans, he knew a little piece of *every* human's Name, enabling him to Command ordinary mortals to sleep, or forget, or fail to see what was right in front of them, so that he had once walked unnoticed and unhindered wherever he wished.

Most of those powers had deserted him now. He still knew the Names of wind, fire, and earth, but without the full power of Faerie to draw on, he could not make them obey him.

But he could still Command mortals if need be . . . and he knew just the mortal to Command.

Keith Pritchard.

He reached out a hand and touched a glowing yellow button.

"Gwen," he said, "please get our district sales manager for Regina on the phone."

3

"THE POWER BE YOURS"

WALLY STRUGGLED up the water staircase, feeling as if he were trapped in a nightmare. The stairs were still there, but losing their form. And they were as slippery as ice—with every step Wally felt in danger of sliding back down to the bottom, into that impossible chamber under the water, with that impossible talking statue made of water. *The Lady of the Lake?* he thought incredulously. *Really?*

But disbelief took a back seat to his most immediate problem, which was that he didn't know how to swim.

The water, clear as crystal a moment before, turned brown and began to foam. The rectangle of sky he'd been struggling for was an arm's length above him. He was almost out . . .

And then the steps vanished, the walls disappeared, and Wascana Lake roared in to fill the void.

Wally floundered in foul-tasting water. He kicked frantically and managed to pop his head above the surface for an instant, catching a glimpse of the boulders by the parking lot before the weight of his clothes dragged him under again. A strangely detached portion of his mind noted that his earlier question about whether the lake was deep enough to drown in was about to be answered.

Another kick. His head burst into the air again, and he desperately gulped a breath, then managed to squeak out, "Help . . .!" But the water sucked him under again, and this time, when he kicked and flailed, he couldn't find his way back to the surface in the foam and scum and brown muddy soup created by the collapse of the magical chamber.

His lungs cried out for air. *I'm drowning*, he thought, disbelieving. *I'm drowning in Wascana Lake . . .*

. . . Mom and Dad will sue them for making it deeper a few years ago . . .

. . . and then something grabbed him. Panic-stricken, he clutched it, pulling it down with him. When he realized it must be Ariane, he forced himself to go limp. Just when he thought he couldn't bear it a moment longer, his head broke through the surface. Ariane struck out for the shore, and within seconds both of them were belly-down in the mud by the parking lot boulders, coughing and spitting.

"Thanks," Wally choked out. "I can't swim."

"I noticed." Ariane rolled over, sat up, and stared at the lake. Wally followed her gaze. Aside from a spot of water muddier than the rest, there was no sign of the Lady's underwater lair.

Maybe I dreamed it, Wally thought. *Or hallucinated it. Maybe it was a . . . what's that old hippie phrase? . . . a "bad trip."*

But he'd never done drugs. And neither dreams nor

hallucinations left you soaking wet, muddy, or stinking. Which left only one other possibility:

It had really happened. Impossibly, incredibly, in defiance of everything he knew about science *and* history, he and Ariane had seen—had spoken to—the Lady of the Lake.

He turned to Ariane. "We need to talk." He looked down at himself. "And change." He sniffed. "And shower."

"I can't go home looking like this," Ariane said.

Wally checked his watch, which somewhat to his surprise still worked. Unlike his malfunctioning and now-lost smartphone. "We can go to my house. There won't be anyone there. My sister always leaves early to meet up with her friends before school. You can change into some of her clothes while we wash yours. You're about the same size."

Ariane blinked. "You have a sister?"

"Yeah. You've met her." His mouth twitched into a half-smile. "Her name's Flish—uh, Felicia. She's a friend of Shania's."

Ariane's eyes widened. "*She's* your sister?"

"Yeah." He shrugged. "Sorry. You can't choose your family."

Her smile surprised him. "You're inviting me to go into Felicia's bedroom and borrow her clothes?"

He felt a sudden pang of trepidation. "Uh, yeah, I guess . . ."

Her smile widened. "Wouldn't pass up that chance for the world." The smile vanished. "But what about school?"

"Aren't you suspended?"

"For you, not me."

He glanced down at himself. "I can't go like this anyway." He looked up again, grinning. "And fortunately, I have the perfect excuse." He held up his right wrist. "Fencing injury. I have a note and everything. I'm in excruciating pain. Couldn't possibly sit through classes."

"You're not even wearing the bandage you had on in the office yesterday," Ariane pointed out.

"Well, true, but they can't see that over the phone." He shrugged. "Anyway, it's at home. I'll put it on for Monday."

Ariane smiled again. Wally decided he liked her smile. "If I'm going home with you," she said, "shouldn't you at least tell me your name?"

"Wally," he said. "Wally Knight."

"Well, Wally Knight, lead on."

DRIPPING and making squelching noises with every step, Ariane followed the unexpected Wally as he wheeled his bicycle west along the bike path. The mist had lifted from the lake, and the morning sun sparkled on the water. A few joggers and dog-walkers gave the dripping duo puzzled looks, but Wally just smiled at them and kept moving.

They took the pedestrian underpass under the north end of the busy Albert Street bridge, then walked a half-block before turning left into a cul-de-sac whose street-sign labelled it Harrington Mews. Wally kept a wary eye out for neighbours as they made their way up the front walk of his much-grander-than-hers house—complete with stone lions flanking the steps—then, once they were through the big red door, showed Ariane to the upstairs bathroom. He waited outside while she stripped, then took away the soaked and stinking clothes she carefully passed out through the door before heading for the second bathroom in the basement.

Ariane hesitated before stepping into the shower, remembering the strange hallucination that had gripped her that morning. *Don't be silly,* she chided herself. *You can't go the rest of your life without taking a shower.* Besides, a mere hallucination seemed almost homey compared to what had happened since.

She got in and turned on the water. Nothing strange happened, and she leaned against the tiles with relief as the hot water sluicing through her hair and down her back washed away the brown residue from Wascana Lake. She stayed there a long time, unwilling to leave her steamy sanctuary and face what she had just experienced.

Part of her wanted to believe it had been a dream. But dreams faded quickly, whereas everything that had happened in the lake was seared in her memory, clear and indelible, right down to the strange phrase she had heard in her mind when the Lady looked deep into her eyes.

Gadewch y dyfroedd byw ynoch, a chi o fewn y dyfroedd. Y p ˆwer yn eiddo i chi. She didn't recognize the language, much less speak it, but somehow she knew its meaning: *Let the waters live within you, and you within the waters. The power be yours.*

You have the power to defeat him, if you will grasp it, the Lady had said first. "Him" being Merlin. Apparently they were supposed to keep Merlin from getting the shards of Arthur's famous sword Excalibur, remaking it, and using it to take over the world.

Yeah, right, she thought. *And anyway, how am I supposed*

to "grasp" this supposed power? How am I even supposed to know if I want it? Mom didn't.

She remembered her mother coming back to the house, soaked to the skin, changed beyond recognition. If her mother had seen the Lady that night, Ariane could understand why she had seemed so shaken, not in her right mind. But that didn't explain why she had denied Ariane was her daughter, or that she even had a daughter—or why she had run away.

Why did she abandon me?

Ariane sighed. Showering wasn't getting her anything but wet.

She turned off the water and stepped onto the pink fuzzy bathmat—the Knights' bathroom was a bit frilly and *froufrou* for her taste—and only then realized there wasn't a towel to be seen.

"Gee, thanks, Wally," she muttered as she knelt, opening the cabinets under the sink. She found toilet paper, bottles of Mr. Clean, a scrub brush, and several old bath toys, but no towels. "How am I supposed to dry myself off—just wish the water away?"

And then she gasped and jerked backward, losing her footing and falling onto her bare bottom with a floor-shaking thump.

Her *bone-dry* bottom. Like every other square centimetre of her—she raised a hand, jerked it back again—*even my hair!* —her backside was no longer wet.

Wally knocked on the door. "Are you all right in there? Did you fall?"

"I'm . . . I'm fine . . . I just . . ." *Just what?* ". . . slipped."

"Okay." Wally sounded dubious. "Are you almost done?"

"Yeah, I'm done. But there aren't any towels."

"Oh, sorry! I'll get you one. Just a second."

Ariane heard his footsteps move down the hall, and she looked around her while waiting. The water from her body hadn't vanished: instead, it had formed a ring-shaped puddle on the floor where she had been standing. It had . . . fled, as if she really had wished it from her body.

This day is getting weirder and weirder.

"I've got a towel," Wally said from the other side of the door. In the reverse of the dance they'd performed earlier when she'd handed him her clothes, Ariane scooted over to the door, positioned herself carefully out of Wally's line of sight, and eased it open. Wally's hand appeared, holding out a dark green towel. She took it, closed the door, then wrapped the towel around her as best she could. Although it was on the smallish side, at least it covered the embarrassing bits. Her hair looked like she'd stuck her finger in a light socket—not surprising, since she hadn't had a chance to comb it while it was wet.

Using one hand to hold her precarious covering in place, she opened the door with the other and sailed out into the hallway, past Wally. Unlike her, he was at least half-dressed, wearing jeans but no shirt or socks. The ribs stood out on his skinny chest. He blushed waist to crown when he saw her, then after that first glance looked up . . . down . . . sideways . . . anywhere but right at her. "Where's your sister's room?" she said.

"It's . . . uh . . ." Wally made a slight gagging sound, as though he found it hard to form words. "Down the hall. Last door. On the right."

"Thank you." Using her free hand to hold the back of the

towel as low as possible, Ariane walked down the hall with all the dignity she could muster. Once inside Felicia's room, she let the towel fall away.

The bathroom's frilly décor must have represented Felicia's mother's taste, not Felicia's. Cool functionality was her style: dark blue carpet, purple bedding, white walls, and, for decoration, a poster of a tattooed and pierced all-girl band Ariane had never heard of. The dresser and desk were utterly bare, everything tucked out of sight.

"A neat freak," Ariane muttered. "Who would have guessed?" She began digging in Felicia's dresser drawers and closet for clothes. She didn't worry about keeping things tidy. By the time she was done, Felicia's room looked a lot less like a *House & Home* photo spread and a lot more like a going-out-of-business sale at Teen Fashions R Us. Ariane couldn't bring herself to wear any of Felicia's underwear, but she donned a plain white cotton top, a heavy wool sweater, a pair of jeans that probably looked like they were sprayed on when Felicia wore them but were comfortably loose on her, white gym socks, and an expensive-looking pair of runners, only one size too big.

She surveyed the mess she'd made, smiled, then went out into the hall and gently closed the door behind her.

Wally wasn't in sight. Ariane descended to the living room and plopped herself on the overstuffed white-leather couch to wait for him, trying not to think about everything that had happened, but unable to stop. It was impossible. Things like that just didn't happen. She must have been hallucinating—another peculiar vision.

But if she had been, then Wally had been hallucinating right along with her. Because here she was, in his house—in

Felicia's house—wearing Felicia's clothes, while her own were . . .

She frowned. Where were hers, anyway?

She got up and went into the kitchen, decorated in stark black and white. As obsessively neat as the rest of the house, it made the comfortable clutter of Aunt Phyllis's kitchen look like a rummage sale in mid-rummage. A door at the far end led into a utility room, where she could see an open washing machine. A quick look confirmed that both her and Wally's clothes were in there, and when she glanced around, she saw her leather jacket hanging, dripping, from a hook by the door.

She wrinkled her nose as she picked at its sodden sleeve. Soaking wet and stinking, it was something *else* she definitely wouldn't have hallucinated. So somehow, some impossible how, the Lady of the Lake—or someone who *called* herself the Lady of the Lake, at least—had opened up a chamber of water in Wascana Lake, had spoken to them . . .

. . . and expected *them* to reassemble Excalibur before Merlin—Merlin, of all people!—could do so.

She snorted. The Lady of the Lake was all wet in more ways than one if she thought her mumbo-jumbo was going to get Ariane to undertake a wild-goose chase like that. *Mom refused the power. So will I.*

But she thought uneasily of the way the water had fled her body in the bathroom. That seemed to imply she had some of the Lady's power already. Had she *already* accepted it? Some of it, at least? Did that mean she really wanted it—without even knowing what it was?

The thought made her uncomfortable. Ironically, she also felt terribly thirsty. She returned to the kitchen, found a glass in the cupboard above the sink, and turned on the tap, letting it run for a few seconds to get cold. Absentmindedly, she stuck her fingers into the flow of the water to test the temperature.

Rushing and gurgling down the drain and through the trap, and into the sewer pipe, flowing out toward the street to the main sewer line to the—

She gasped and jerked her hand out of the water, and the vision—no, the *sensation*—vanished. For a horrifying instant she had felt as if she were about to pour down the drain with the flowing liquid, dissolving into it as it rushed to lake, river, and sea. She stared at her dripping hand. It trembled. The trembling spread to her arm, to her knees, and then to her whole body. She groped for one of the tall, black stools that ringed the granite-topped island in the middle of the kitchen, and hauled herself onto it before she could collapse where she stood.

WALLY TRIED to act cool when Ariane came out of the shower wearing only a towel . . . an act made more difficult by the fact that he hadn't been able to find a shirt downstairs. He knew he was blushing, and knew there was no way to hide it. Worse, he also knew he looked like a twelve-year-old even though he was almost fifteen, and he hated it. He was owed an adolescent growth spurt, damn it!

Still, even if he couldn't do anything about his scrawny body, he could at least try to be a gentleman and not stare at Ariane's not-scrawny one. He could also try hard not to hope that her towel slipped off before she made it to Felicia's room.

He almost succeeded.

As the closing door hid her from sight, he glanced into the bathroom, and frowned at the floor. "What the . . .?" He bent over and looked at a strange, ring-shaped puddle. The tiling was bone-dry in the centre. He couldn't imagine how it could have formed.

Well, it was hardly the strangest thing that had happened that morning. He went into his own room, where he rummaged in his dresser for clean socks. He tugged them on, then pulled out a T-shirt that bore the words REAL MEN HUNT DEER WITH SWORDS above an image of a leaping deer cut in half. He slipped it on, then picked up his hairbrush. As he met his own gaze in the mirror, he paused, remembering those panic-filled moments when he couldn't keep his head above the lake's surface.

Ariane saved my life. He'd barely met her, but what had happened that morning was so amazing that he felt like he'd known her all his life. He shook his head, ran a brush through his red hair, then padded down the hall and down the stairs.

He found Ariane sitting on one of the stools at the island in the centre of the kitchen, her face pale, cheeks shining with tears.

"What's wrong? You look like you've seen a ghost!" Wally realized the instant he spoke that it was a monumentally stupid thing to say in light of everything that had happened.

"I don't know what I saw. In the lake, or . . ." Ariane

looked at her hand, then wiped it hastily on her borrowed jeans.

"But she told you." Wally clambered onto the stool next to her. "I heard it too. The Lady gave you—gave us!—a quest." He relished that thought. He'd completed hordes of virtual quests, and now he was part of a real one! "To find the shards of Excalibur. 'Seek for the sword that was broken, in Imladris it dwells . . .'" He grinned, savouring the words like a chunk of Belgian chocolate.

"Stop it!" Ariane snapped, voice sharp as a slap. "Just stop it! This isn't *The Lord of the Rings*. This isn't a story. This is . . . I don't know what it is. Maybe it's all a hallucination. Maybe I tripped on the stairs this morning and I'm lying in the hospital with a fractured skull."

"Hallucinations aren't this internally consistent," Wally said. He reached out and pinched her arm.

"Ow!" She jerked it away. For a second she looked as if she would hit him.

Wally raised his hands. "Sorry! But see? No hallucination. Anyway, why on earth would you hallucinate *me*? Why not Elijah Wood?" From her expression, she'd already wondered that. That stung a little, even if he *was* the one who had said it.

"But . . . it *can't* be real," Ariane said, though it sounded as if she was arguing more with herself than with him. "Arthur? Merlin? The Lady of the Lake? Excalibur? They're storybook characters."

"Make up your mind. First you say it isn't a story, then you say it is. You can't have it both ways. I say it's real. I say you're the new Lady of the Lake."

"That can't be!"

"That's what the Lady said—you're her heir. That makes you the Lady of the Lake for the twenty-first century, just like she was for the eleventh or the ninth or whenever the heck she lived. And that means you have a responsibility, a duty." He leaned in close, caught up in the excitement of the thing. "You have to stop Merlin from gathering the shards of Excalibur. It's up to you to save the world." *And I get to help you.* He grinned and leaned back again. "Man, you are so freakin' lucky!"

ARIANE COULDN'T BELIEVE what Wally had just said, couldn't believe he was grinning at her as he said it. "Lucky?" She glared at him. "Lucky?" She stood up. "I may be *going* crazy, but you're already there!"

"You're not crazy. And neither am I. You have to—"

"I don't have to do anything!" Ariane snapped. "Except go home and face the music now that my aunt knows I've been suspended for three days. And next Wednesday, I'll go back to school, and everything will go back to normal."

Wally shook his head. "No, it won't. She gave you something, some kind of power—what was it she said, some kind of magic spell—"

Gadewch y dyfroedd byw ynoch, a chi o fewn y dyfroedd. Y p^wer yn eiddo i chi. The words echoed in Ariane's mind even when she didn't want them to.

"I don't care what she said!" she shouted, trying to drown out the memories of the Lady's voice, of the waters singing to her, of the dreams of a sword in the water, of the wishing away of the water on her body, of the sensation of rushing away with the running water down the drain. "It's all crap! She can go to hell!"

She leaped up so violently her stool fell over. Wally jumped off his own to avoid being hit by it. Both stools crashed behind her as she ran out, throwing open the front door so hard it bounced and banged shut again behind her.

A group of girls appeared at the mouth of the cul-de-sac just as she reached it. Half-blinded by tears, she dashed through them, careening off of someone who didn't move out of her way fast enough. "Hey! Stop!" one of them shouted, but she kept running.

An instant later she realized who the girls had been: Shania and Felicia's little gang, probably cutting class—and heading to Felicia's house.

Wally!

She shoved aside her momentary pang of guilt. She didn't want to think about Wally. She didn't want to think at all.

It was all too much. Two and a half years ago, everything had been fine, everything had been normal, she'd been just another seventh-grader, recently turned thirteen, looking forward to being a teenager at last . . . now her mom was gone, her old friends were gone, her old life was gone, and she was supposed to save the world? Throw away every last vestige of normality, her final chance to be just one more kid in a sea of kids and become some kind of freak instead?

She ran until her legs and breath gave out. Back in Wascana Park, she doubled over, gasping for breath, then straightened, leaned against a tree, and slid down its rough trunk to the brown grass beneath it. Out of sight of the lake—

she didn't want to see the lake again—and out of sight of passersby as well, she buried her head in her folded arms.

When her heartbeat had slowed and she could draw her breath more easily, she raised her head and looked at her watch. Apparently it really *was* waterproof: it was still running, and told her it was just after nine in the morning.

It seemed incredible that so little time had passed since she had first heard the singing of the water.

Running hadn't changed anything. She couldn't run away from reality, and as fantastic as it seemed, her reality now included the Lady of the Lake. She had no choice but to confront the ordeal, and now that she was alone and slowly calming down, she thought perhaps she could. She took a deep breath, closed her eyes, and thought back to that morning's encounter.

Her mother had met the Lady, too. That seemed clear. And refused the power the Lady had offered her. And then . . . for whatever reason . . . she had run away: not only from the Lady and her proffered power, but from Ariane as well.

And then, tentatively, another thought took shape in her mind, a thought she hardly dared to put into words, for fear it would evaporate into nothing more than wishful thinking if she held it up to the light. But it wouldn't go away, and at last she dared to let it rise to the surface: *With the Lady's power, I might be able to find Mom.*

She told herself not to be an idiot, not to let herself get sucked in by false hope. No one had been able to figure out what had happened to her mom, not the police, not Aunt Phyllis, not the media. She'd tried to accept that, tried to accept that her mother was gone forever . . .

But if I can use magic . . .

She blinked away sudden tears as a surge of hope threatened to overwhelm her. *Even if the power is real, there's no guarantee you can use it to find Mom,* she told herself, fighting to stay sensible. *She may not be out there to find. She may be dead. Everyone thinks she is. Everyone . . .*

. . . everyone except me! And with that fierce inward shout of defiance, she let the faint flicker of hope burst into a white-hot flame that for the moment, at least, burned away all her doubts.

For you, Mom, Ariane thought fiercely. *Not for the Lady, but for you, I'll accept the Lady's power—whatever it is!*

For a moment nothing happened. Then the bright October sunlight shining all around her became cold and watery, as if she were beneath the surface of the lake again, looking up through rippling water. Though she knew she was alone, she heard the Lady's voice from close behind her: *Gadewch y dyfroedd byw ynoch, a chi o fewn y dyfroedd. Y pŵer yn eiddo i chi . . . Let the waters live within you, and you within the waters. The power be yours.*

"The power be mine!" Ariane whispered.

The sense that the Lady stood right behind her lasted a few seconds longer, then faded. The sunlight regained its normal strength. She took a deep, shuddering breath as the everyday world reasserted itself. A motorcycle roared along the winding park road, and from the playground she heard the distant shrieks and squeals of small children.

In some ways, nothing had changed. She was still suspended from school, and she still had to go home and face the consequences, just like any other teenager in trouble. But unlike any other teenager, she had a quest—not a video game quest, but a real life-and-death quest.

An impossible quest, Ariane thought. *I need to learn everything I can about Excalibur, Merlin and the Lady of the Lake.*

She couldn't go home to her own computer, and she had to spend the day somewhere. She got to her feet and set off on the five-block walk to the central branch of the Regina Public Library.

4

"IF I WERE YOU, I'D RUN"

AT THE JUST-OPENED LIBRARY, Ariane found an unoccupied computer and searched the Web until she thought her eyes would fall out of her head. But even after four hours of Googling, she didn't feel much wiser. Millions of words had been written about Arthur, Excalibur and the Lady of the Lake, and all of the accounts contradicted each other. What was truth, and what was fiction?

It was early afternoon when she left the library for the nearby Cornwall Centre mall. She bought a copy of *Asimov's Science Fiction Magazine* at the magazine store she passed along the way, and read the book reviews and one of the short stories while eating a giant slice of second-rate pepperoni pizza in the mall food court. After that she poked through stores, and returned to the food court for a fruit smoothie. As the mall filled up with workers on their way home, she knew she couldn't delay it any longer.

She had to face Aunt Phyllis.

Twenty minutes later she stood on their porch, hesitating

and trying to figure out the best way to deal with her aunt. She might be able to delay the inevitable if she could get to her room before Aunt Phyllis realized she was home . . . but when she opened the front door, her aunt was standing between her and the staircase, arms folded, face pinched into a frown. "Ariane Elizabeth Forsythe, you stop right there!"

Ariane didn't have much choice, short of knocking Aunt Phyllis down.

"I received a phone call from the school quite early this morning," her aunt continued. "From Mr. Stanton." She unfolded her arms. In one hand she held the pink notepad that usually lay beside the phone. She nodded sharply to flick the reading glasses perched on her head down onto her nose, then peered through them at the paper. "He informed me that my niece and legal ward, Ariane Forsythe, 'has been suspended for three days for fighting, and is not to return to school until next Wednesday, at which time she must report to the office to arrange for mandatory counselling.'" Aunt Phyllis lowered the pad and glared at Ariane. "Mr. Stanton said you attacked a girl in the hallway yesterday after school. Is that true?"

She started it, Ariane wanted to say, but realized she'd sound like a petulant little kid. "Yes."

Aunt Phyllis's eyes widened. "You admit it?"

I just did, didn't I? Ariane fought the anger kindling inside her and kept her voice steady. "Yes."

Aunt Phyllis's face flushed. "No explanation? No excuses?"

Ariane didn't want to drag Aunt Phyllis into her war with Wally's sister and her friends. The last thing she needed was her aunt storming into the school demanding to see the principal. Things were bad enough without getting labelled a crybaby.

"No."

"Ariane, how could you?" Aunt Phyllis's voice, suffused with anger and disappointment, grated on Ariane's nerves like fingernails on a blackboard. "You promised me you'd changed." *Scrape . . . scrape . . . scrape.* "You promised me you wouldn't get into trouble like you did at your other schools. Is this how you keep your promise? What would your mother say?"

Ariane's relative calm, teeth-clenched though it was, vanished. She barely recognized her own voice as she yelled, "You leave Mom out of this! This has nothing to do with her."

Pendragon, who had just started down the stairs to greet her, hissed.

Aunt Phyllis's eyes blazed. "I will not. I'm your legal guardian. I wish to God your mother were still here, but she's not. And I—"

"Don't talk about her like she's dead! She's not dead!"

"Maybe not. But she might as well be. She's not here, and she's not coming back. And you have to face that fact. I'm sorry for you, I'm sorry you have to grow up so early, but that's the way it is. I miss her as much as you do—"

"That's a lie. She's my mother. You can't possibly miss her as much as—"

"The hell I can't!" Aunt Phyllis's voice began to tremble. "Emily was—*is*—my baby sister. I practically raised her after our mother died. I never thought I'd have to raise her daughter too. But she's gone, and she left you to me to look after, and now

I find out I'm apparently not doing a very good job. But you know what? That just means I'm going to have to try harder." She drew herself up to her full height, still half a head shorter than Ariane. "You're grounded, young lady. For a month."

"A month? That's not fair!"

"Fair or not, that's the way it's going to be." Aunt Phyllis stepped aside. "Go to your room. We can talk about this in a more civilized fashion after you've had a chance to cool down."

"'Go to your room!'" Ariane mimicked savagely. "'You're grounded, young lady.' You're treating me like a child. I'm almost sixteen. Do you realize that?"

"I'm through arguing. Go to your room. Now!"

"Go to hell!" Ariane spun on her heel and crashed out through the front door into the gathering autumn twilight.

"Ariane!" she heard Aunt Phyllis shout, but she didn't look back. She thought she might explode. She wanted to break something, crush something, punch someone. Instead, she ran down the front walk and up the street, brushing past some girl on the sidewalk who was turned away from her, talking into a phone. After a few more steps, Arian realized that she was heading for the same place she had sought refuge that morning—the lake.

Her kingdom, if the Lady could be believed. Though at that moment, she didn't want a kingdom.

She wanted sanctuary.

WALLY HAD NEVER HAD A MORE unpleasant shock in his fourteen years than the one he received a few minutes after Ariane ran out.

He was in the utility room, getting ready to wash their lake-soaked clothes. He had just poured in the soap and closed the lid when he heard the front door open. *She came back*, he thought with great relief. "Ariane?" he shouted. "I'm in here."

He turned around—and came face to face with his sister, whose glare was hot enough to melt lead. Her voice, on the other hand, could have frozen air. "What was *she* doing here?"

Wally's first impulse, to play dumb, *was* dumb. Felicia had probably seen Ariane leaving the house. "She . . . had an accident. On the way to school. She . . . needed to clean up."

"She was wearing my clothes!"

"Well, she had to wear something." Wally cast a longing gaze at the door into the kitchen, thinking of escape . . . and saw Shania, leaning against the kitchen counter. Muffled voices from the living room revealed the presence of . . . Buffy? Heather? What *were* those girls' names . . . ?

"You let her into my room?" Felicia's voice turned sharp as an icicle.

"My clothes are too small." *Shut up, Wally*, he warned himself. *You're not helping.*

"Shut up, Wally," Felicia snapped. Apparently she agreed. She grabbed his arm, spun him around, pinned his wrist against his shoulder blades, and frog-marched him out of the utility room.

Shania didn't even look away from the glitter she was brushing onto her fingernails. "So what's up?"

"My little *brother*—" Felicia made him sound like something green and furry she'd found growing on leftovers—"let that foster brat into my room. He told her," she yanked his wrist higher, making him gasp, "that she could wear my clothes."

Shania held out her left hand and wriggled the fingers, admiring her handiwork. "What happened to hers?"

Felicia jerked her head at the utility room. "In the washing machine."

Shania straightened up, and grinned—or, at least, showed her teeth. It made her look like a shark. "I'll get them for her. We'll want to return them, won't we?"

"Yeah." Felicia bared her teeth in turn. "We will."

"Shouldn't we all be getting to school?" Wally said hopefully.

"Shut up," Felicia snapped, but Shania turned her shark-like smile toward him.

"Somebody set off a stink bomb in the chemistry lab before the first bell even rang. Classes are cancelled for the rest of the day."

At least that explained why they were here, at home, where he'd thought he'd be safe. *If I ever find the guy who made that stink bomb . . .*

Shania turned toward the living room. "Stephanie! Cassandra!"

Oh, yeah, Wally thought. *That's it. Stephanie and Cassan*—"Ow!" he yelped as Felicia pushed him toward the stairs. She forced him up to the second floor while Shania started to issue orders downstairs.

"Get over to Ariane's house. Wallace Street, remember? Both of you. Keep watch. All day if you have to—you can spell each other off. The minute you see her, call me. If she's going in, stay put and wait. If she's coming out, follow her."

"What are we going to do to her?" Stephanie—or was it Cassandra?—asked, but Wally didn't have a chance to hear the answer. By then, Felicia was propelling him down the hallway toward her room.

So Wally repeated the question to his sister. "What are you going to do to Ariane?"

Instead of answering, she released him and shoved him hard against the wall. His head hit with a dull thud. "Ow!" Rubbing his skull, he turned just in time to see Felicia open the door to her room.

Her mouth fell open. "Oh . . . my . . . God!" Each word was two notes higher and ten decibels louder than the one before. Wally, feeling his head for a bump, peered around her, and gaped.

It looked like every piece of clothing Felicia owned had been pulled from its place in the dresser or closet and tossed on the floor. Wally felt an urge to laugh that could only be classified as insane—in the mood Felicia was in, she'd undoubtedly kill him.

"Sorry," he managed to say, hoping he sounded believably contrite. "I didn't know—"

"Shut up!" Felicia grabbed him and shoved him into her room. He fell again and slid, on a pile of panties, a metre across the carpet. "I want this room to look exactly the way it did when I left it this morning, or so help me—"

"Okay, okay," Wally muttered. "I'll take care of it."

"You do that. And *we'll* take care of Ariane!"

She slammed the door. Wally sighed and got to his feet. *This is not,* he thought as he picked up a purple sock and began casting around for its mate, *a propitious beginning to our quest.*

He glanced out the window. Cassandra and Stephanie were just turning the corner of the block. It was too late to follow them to Ariane's house, and unlike them, he didn't know Ariane's address. (He wondered how *they* did. *Maybe as head witch of the coven, Shania asked her good friend Satan for assistance,* he thought.) He didn't even know Ariane's aunt's name. He had no way to warn her. All he could do was wait to find out what happened.

He heard voices downstairs. Felicia and Shania were still in the living room, and that meant the only safe place for him was . . . right here.

He spotted the second purple sock, hanging from the desk lamp. He grabbed it, folded it with its mate, then leaned over and picked up a frilly black bra.

At least he had plenty to keep him occupied.

By THE TIME Ariane reached the empty parking lot by the lake it was almost dark, and much colder. She hugged herself tightly. Her anger still burned, but it didn't provide much warmth, and it was beginning to be tempered by guilt. *I'll go back soon.* She had to: she had nowhere else to go.

She walked to the boulder where she had been sitting when she first heard the water calling her. She sat down on it again and stared at the lake a smooth, silver sheet that reflected the twilight sky. She heard a car pull into the parking lot. Lights swept over her, briefly illuminating the naked trees on Willow Island. Ariane hunched her shoulders and hoped whoever it was would leave her alone.

A car door slammed, then another. Now footsteps were crunching toward her—too many to be one person. Ariane still didn't turn around. Wascana Lake, right in the heart of the city, was always popular with people out for a stroll, but why these annoying strollers had chosen this particular moment—

"Well, well, well. If it isn't Airy-Anne, out enjoying the fresh air."

Ariane slowly turned her head. Four girls stood behind her. *Hail, hail, the gang's all here,* she thought. She saw Shania, but Felicia seemed to be in charge for the moment. She was carrying a plastic shopping bag. "Those are my clothes you're wearing, Airy-Anne." She opened the bag and tossed the contents onto the ground in Ariane's direction. "*These* are yours."

The black shirt and jeans Ariane had been wearing that morning, still filthy and unwashed, landed with a sodden thump. So did her leather jacket. Someone had slashed the sleeves and lining beyond repair.

Anger surged in her again. Keeping her eyes on the gang, she rose to her feet. The four girls had her trapped between the parking lot and Wascana's cold water. A red Toyota SUV idled behind them. Its exhaust puffed out into the chill, still air, glowing golden under the parking lot's sodium-vapour lights. "It was very sweet of you to loan them to me," she said.

"You mean it was very stupid of my brother," Felicia growled. She crumpled up the shopping bag she'd brought Ariane's clothes in and tossed it to one side. *At least I don't have to worry about getting Wally in trouble,* Ariane thought. *He's already in it.*

"Your brother's very nice, *Flish*." She remembered that Wally had told her his sister hated that nickname. "Amazingly enough."

"My brother," Felicia snarled, "is a geek loser who should learn to keep his pimply nose out of my business—and out of my room." She took a step closer. "I want my clothes back, Airy-Anne."

"I'll mail them to you." She stepped off the boulder in the direction of the parking lot—she needed room to manoeuvre.

Felicia grabbed her arm. "I want them *now*."

Ariane jerked free, but someone else grabbed her from behind. She opened her mouth to scream, but a hand clamped over her lips. A moment later, someone jammed a twisted scarf between her teeth and tied it around her head so tightly she thought her cheeks would split. She struggled, but the two girls holding her forced her down onto her back and pinned her arms to the ground. She kicked as hard as she could, just missing Felicia's shin.

Felicia's eyes glittered yellow in the sodium light. "Strip her."

Ariane's anger swelled to rage. A distant roaring began, and grew louder. There was something familiar about it.

The girls lifted her up and forced one arm out of the sweater sleeve, then the other, then peeled the sweater over her head. She kicked again, this time landing a solid blow on Felicia's knee, but the girls threw her back to the ground. Felicia swore and limped backward. "The jeans!" she snapped.

"Felicia, are you sure . . ." Ariane recognized Shania's voice, and knew her first instinct had been correct. Felicia was in charge this time—maybe from this time on. The other two girls didn't pay any attention to Shania's concerned query. One of them sat on Ariane's legs to keep her from kicking, and tugged off first one shoe, then the other.

The roaring in Ariane's mind crescendoed and grew more distinct, and at last she recognized it. Four years ago, when she was eleven, her mom had taken her to Toronto. While they were there they had driven down to Niagara Falls. *That* was where she had heard that sound before—it was the earthshaking thunder of countless tonnes of water hurtling over a cliff, falling, pounding against the rocks far below.

But this time, Ariane heard something new mingled with that thunder: a joyful chanting, solemn and powerful in its own way. It was the song of the water she had heard only hours before, the call of—or maybe *to*—the Lady of the Lake.

She dimly felt her socks being pulled off, the cold air flowing around her bare feet.

Felicia held up her cell phone. "Two seconds after you're naked, the pictures are going to be hitting the phone of every kid in my contact list," Felicia said. "You're about to become the most famous girl in Oscana Collegiate, Airy-Anne."

The girl sitting on Ariane's knees turned herself around and began fumbling with the button of Ariane's jeans. Ariane hardly noticed. Her attention was turned inward, seeking the source of that thunderous song. It was like following an unfamiliar path through a dark, dripping rain forest, trying to find a view of the sea. She was close, so close . . .

Jeans unbuttoned and unzipped. Hands in the waist-band, about to pull them off.

"Wait, get her to her feet first," Felicia said. "Stephanie, you pull the t-shirt over her head. Cassandra, pull the jeans down from behind. That way neither of you will be in the shot."

Almost . . . almost . . .

They hauled her to her feet. In a moment she'd be standing naked before Felicia's cell phone lens.

And then, with an almost physical shock, as though she'd stuck her finger in an electrical socket, she connected with the power she had sensed building inside of her.

Gadewch y dyfroedd byw ynoch, a chi o fewn y dyfroedd. Y p ˆwer yn eiddo i chi!

The Lady's voice echoed in her head with the force of waves breaking against a rocky shore.

Let the waters live within you, and you within the waters. The power be yours!

And it *was* hers, at last. Here was the epiphany she had missed before: power she had never imagined, suddenly at her beck and call. All the water in Wascana Lake felt like a part of her body. She could sense everything in it, locate every fish, every rock, every sunken bicycle and pop can and grocery cart. The water lived in her and she in it—and she could use it as she willed.

And she willed . . . *this.*

The lake erupted. Ropes of water like muddy snakes shot skyward, poised above her and her tormentors. Felicia, Shania, Stephanie, and Cassandra froze like hares caught in a car's headlights. Ariane pulled free of Stephanie's slack-ened grip, ripped the gag from her mouth, and waded three steps into the lake. The water, though it had to be ice-cold, felt as warm as a blanket around her bare feet.

"If I were you," she said, "I'd run."

The girls stared at her in confusion, faces yellow in the lamplight.

And then Ariane struck.

The watery ropes, black with rotting muck, sank back toward the surface of the lake, thickening, crouching, and trembling like feral cats—and then sprang toward the shore with the force of a water cannon. The first struck Felicia in the chest, knocking her off her feet, rolling her over and over across the parking lot. The other girls turned to run, but it was too late. The blasts of mud-choked water hit their backs instead of their chests, throwing them to the pavement.

Screaming, they tried to scramble to their feet, but Ariane wasn't finished.

Thinner, cleaner tentacles of water reached out from the lake and snapped down on the cowering girls like whips. One smashed Felicia's cell phone, and glittering shards of plastic and circuitry scattered across the asphalt. Other tendrils struck the girls with audible cracks, leaving red marks on their bare skin. Weeping and shrieking, the girls ran for the Toyota. A tendril of water smashed in the back window, scattering shards of shining glass across the pavement. The SUV skidded out of the parking lot before the doors even closed.

Ariane raised her hands and the tendrils of water slipped back into the lake, leaving behind only a few flecks of foam. She turned to face the once-more placid water. "Thank you," she whispered.

The roaring had subsided, but she could feel it, tucked

away, ready to be called upon if she ever needed it again. *This* was the power the Lady had bequeathed to her. Ariane needed to study it, to understand it . . .

A fit of shivering gripped her, so strong her teeth clattered like castanets. Her feet suddenly felt as if she'd stuck them in a deep freezer, and a wave of tiredness washed over her. She was exhausted. She needed to go home, fast.

She buttoned her jeans and zipped them up again. The shoes, socks, and sweater the gang had stripped off her lay soaked in the parking lot. Ariane knelt and touched them. The water sprang away on her command, and she gratefully pulled on the now-dry sweater. As she was tugging on the equally dry shoes and socks, a lone jogger passed through the parking lot, glancing at her as if wondering what nut would go wading in the lake in this weather.

She gave him her most innocent smile, gathered her own filthy clothes, stuffed them in the shopping bag Felicia had brought them in, and headed home.

She had plans to make.

WALLY WAS SUPPOSED to be doing homework in the living room (but was actually watching TV) when Felicia came in that night. Once he had finished tidying her room, he'd stayed upstairs until he heard Felicia and Shania leave. When he did come downstairs, he discovered that they'd taken Ariane's clothes, still unwashed, with them.

His presence in the house had been an unpleasant surprise for Ms. Carson when she'd arrived around three. She didn't believe his story of a stink bomb in the chemistry lab until she called the school and confirmed it herself. Fortunately, she didn't think to ask if he'd been at school at all.

He hoped Ariane would send some kind of message, but the house phone didn't ring, nobody knocked on the door, and the only e-mails he received promised him cut-rate prescription drugs and a significant portion of a Nigerian ex-politician's fortune.

At five-thirty he ate his spaghetti under the baleful glare of Ms. Carson, who somehow made it clear, without saying a word, that she considered it *his* fault Felicia hadn't come home yet. After supper he retired to the living room with a Coke and a plate of Oreos, while Ms. Carson banged around in the kitchen for a while. Before she left for one of her committee meetings—Save Our Squirrels or Protectors of the Park or something like that—she warned him sternly to tell his sister where the leftover spaghetti was when she came in. "She'll need to eat after a hard night of studying with her friends. You tell her, now."

"I promise." Wally didn't try to disabuse Ms. Carson of the fanciful notion that Felicia had been studying.

About a quarter to seven, more than half an hour after the sun had set, Wally heard the front door open and close. He only caught a glimpse of Felicia as she passed the living room door on the way to the stairs, but what he saw was enough to make him jump to his feet and rush after her.

He reached the bottom of the stairs just as his sister disappeared along the upstairs hallway. He looked at the front door, and then up the steps.

A clear trail of black, wet spots marked Felicia's passage.

He ran upstairs. She was in the bathroom, T-shirt half-off. Stinking water and black muck soaked her from head to foot—just as it had soaked him and Ariane that morning. On her chest, just below her bra, he saw a big purpling bruise.

He gaped at her. "What happened to you?"

She jerked her T-shirt back down. "Don't you ever knock?" she snarled.

"You left the bathroom door open."

"I didn't know you were here. Now get out."

He didn't budge. "You're soaked. Wascana Lake, from the smell of it. Fall in?"

"None of your business." She pointed to the door. "Get out!"

"All right, all right." He backed up, and she slammed the door in his face. He put his mouth close to the door. "Ariane put up a fight, eh?"

The door opened again so suddenly he jumped back. "You shut up about her!" Felicia's voice shook and her green eyes blazed in her pale face. He'd never seen her so angry. "You don't mention her. And you don't talk to her. If I catch you—"

"You're dripping all over the carpet," Wally pointed out.

Felicia told him to do something to himself that would have shocked Ms. Carson into a dead faint, then slammed the door again. A moment later he heard water running in the shower.

Wally returned to his homework and the TV, but couldn't pay attention to either. Instead, he stared into a corner of the room at nothing in particular. Felicia had gone after Ariane. Felicia had come back bruised, and as wet and furious as a half-drowned cat.

The conclusion was inescapable. Somehow—he had no idea how—Ariane had gotten the better of his sister.

He grinned. The more he learned about Ariane, the more he liked her.

The fact that he and she had a magical quest to complete was just gravy.

☙   5   ❧

THE WHITE FORD

BY THE TIME Ariane got home to Wallace Street, she was more exhausted than she could remember ever having been in her life. Her determination to explore her strange new power and think seriously about how she could use it to fulfill the Lady's quest—and use it to find her mother—had given way to an even stronger determination to go straight to bed.

Nevertheless, for some reason the College Avenue intersection drew her tired attention. She stared at it, frowning. For a moment, nothing moved. Then a white Ford Focus turned the corner. It drove slowly past her, and as it passed, she caught a glimpse of its driver, a middle-aged man with a greying beard and ponytail. He didn't see her—he was looking at something in the passenger seat. The car continued down the street and turned left at the next intersection.

Ariane stared after it. She'd never seen that car in the neighbourhood before. There was nothing particularly odd about *that*. The driver could be visiting someone. He could have been looking down at a map in the driver's seat. But still, something about the car and the driver felt wrong in a way Ariane couldn't quite put her finger on. *The Lady's power, warning me about something?*

She shook her head. Most likely, Aunt Phyllis's paranoia about prowlers was starting to rub off on her.

Pulling her house key from her pocket, she walked by the tipsy garden gnome and back up the front steps she had dashed down in fury just an hour ago. The outer door was unlocked, and she stepped into the little entryway. But she paused before unlocking the inner door, gathering her strength to confront her aunt yet again.

She knew she needed to talk to Aunt Phyllis, to smooth things over, but right now what she needed most was sleep. She would have to convince her aunt to put off their heart-to-heart until tomorrow. Wouldn't it be better to talk after they had both had a good night's sleep? Silently composing her argument in her head, Ariane took a deep breath, unlocked the door, and opened it.

No one called out to her. In fact, she could hear nothing but the muttering voice of some CBC commentator on the radio.

Ariane crept forward and looked through the French doors into the living room. Aunt Phyllis sat in her favourite chair, head thrown back, face slack and mouth slightly open. For a horrible moment, Ariane thought she was dead, that their argument had triggered a heart attack or a stroke. Then she saw Aunt Phyllis's chest rising and falling. *She must have dozed off waiting for me to come home.*

Sleep had smoothed some of the lines in Aunt Phyllis's

face, and Ariane could see a hint of her mother's features there—a strong enough hint that her breath caught in her throat. "Mom," she whispered. "Where are you?"

The moment passed. The woman in the chair was just Aunt Phyllis: a small, vulnerable woman, trying to do her best in a horribly difficult situation. Ashamed of her earlier outburst, and resolving to put things right in the morning, Ariane pulled a pink and green flowered afghan from the couch, spread it over her aunt, and then tiptoed up to her room.

She spotted Pendragon asleep on her bed just as she was about to close the door, so she left it open a crack to keep the cat from waking her up in the middle of the night scratching to be let out. She pulled her dirty clothes out of the shopping bag and stuffed them down the laundry chute. The leather jacket was a write-off, but she couldn't quite bear to throw it away yet; instead, she tossed it over her desk chair. She stripped off the clothes she had borrowed from Felicia, wadded them into a lump and kicked them into a corner, then tugged on her warmest flannel pyjamas and climbed into bed, careful not to disturb Pendragon.

She was so exhausted she expected the night to zip by in deep, dreamless slumber. And with Pendragon's solid little body providing a comforting warm lump against her back, she fell asleep almost instantly.

But in the middle of the night, she dreamed a new dream . . .

A LAKE the colour of copper. The sun a blood-red ball, low in a sky thick with smoke and fog. Fires burning up and down the shore. Red-tinged water lapping red-tinged mud, and in the mud, the broken bodies of men: slashed, dismembered, disembowelled, headless. Wind moaning through barren trees and dying men moaning in the mire.

Out of the mist lurched a man in chain mail, white tunic torn, armour, clothes, face, long golden hair and thick blond beard splattered with mud and blood. More blood welled over the fingers of his left hand, pressed tightly to a wound in his side. His right arm dragged a sword that gleamed silver and gold even in the dim, hellish light.

The wounded man staggered through the churned mud, weaving through and stepping over the bodies of men and horses, until his feet splattered water. He took a deep breath, then another, then drew himself up and turned. He spun once, twice, three times, and the third time released the sword, falling to his knees as the blade hurtled out over the lake.

It flew an impossibly long distance, as though something in the lake were pulling it. But Ariane could no longer see the scene on the shore. She was suddenly underwater, rising toward the surface. Her arm, clad in white damask filigreed with silver and studded with pearls, reached into the cold air. The sword whirled toward her, flashing in the light. Her fingers closed around the red leather and fine gold wire that wrapped the hilt, and she drew the blade into the water. She sank into green-tinged darkness, holding the sword at arm's length, but even as the light faded, the sword gleamed silver and gold, as brightly as if the noonday sun shone upon it.

ARIANE WOKE with her heart racing. She lay in the darkness for a moment, staring at the ceiling, then sat up. The light from the hallway no longer shone through the crack in the door. Aunt Phyllis must have gone to bed.

She recognized the dream from her library research. The wounded man must have been Gawain, or Bevidere, or whatever his name had really been, the last of Arthur's knights left standing after Mordred dealt the King his deathblow at the battle of Camlann. At the King's command, he had thrown Excalibur into the water, returning it to the Lady of the Lake.

My ancestor, Ariane thought. She remembered the blast of black muddy water rolling Felicia across the parking lot like a rag doll. *And now me.*

But something else was tugging at her mind, a strange sensation, almost like an itch. *Something's happening outside . . .*

Unable to help herself, she went to the window and peered through the blinds.

The white Ford Focus was parked across the street. A vivid blue glow filled the front seat, and against the glow, she saw the dark silhouette of the ponytailed man.

Pendragon hissed, and Ariane looked down to see the cat standing in the windowsill, back arched, every hair standing on end, glaring at the blue-lit car with shining green eyes.

The glow vanished. A moment later the Focus's lights illuminated the empty street, and it drove away.

Pendragon sat down and began to lick himself furiously, flattening his ruffled fur. Ariane watched the car's taillights dwindle toward College Avenue, then turn left. The driver didn't bother signalling. *Someone knows,* she thought. *Someone knows I've seen the Lady.*

And she could think of only one someone who it could be: Merlin. Was that ponytailed figure in the front seat the ancient wizard himself?

In a Ford Focus? she thought, bemused. *Wouldn't he at least go for a . . . a Jaguar? Or maybe that car James Bond drives—an Aston Martin?*

She shivered despite her flannel pyjamas and went back to bed, pulling the covers up over her head as she had when she was little and thought monsters lurked in her closet. For a long time she lay awake, listening to her own heartbeat, wondering about the man in the car and what would happen next . . . but she was worn out from the day's events, and, slowly, she slipped back into sleep, where no new dreams troubled her.

When she woke up and pushed away the covers, she saw sunlight falling on the spruce tree in the front yard. She'd slept late: this time of year the sun didn't reach the spruce until ten-thirty or eleven in the morning. She could hear the faint sound of radio voices downstairs. Aunt Phyllis was up and about.

First things first. She took off her pyjamas, belted on her dressing gown, and made her way to the bathroom. She hesitated for just a moment before washing her hands, afraid of what might happen when she touched the water, but the only result was her hands got wet. She soaped, rinsed and dried them, then started the shower. Again, she hesitated before stepping into it, but again, nothing happened.

Has the power left me?

But—no. She could feel it, coiled deep inside her, ready

to spring to life. And she knew, somehow, that now *she* was in control. She exerted a small portion of that power, and the water curved away from her body, forming a curtain of falling droplets around her. She relaxed her control, and the water streamed down her skin again. She repeated the exercise, marvelling at the sheer impossibility of it. *I wonder what else I can do?* For the first time, she almost relished the thought of finding out. She finished her shower and got dressed, then took a deep breath and headed downstairs.

Aunt Phyllis was loading the dishwasher, her back to the door. She had just lifted a coffee mug from the sink when Ariane stepped into the kitchen. The floor creaked beneath her weight. Aunt Phyllis froze. Then, without turning around, she finished putting the mug in the dishwasher and reached for a dirty plate.

"Aunt Phyllis." The words came out in a croak. Ariane cleared her throat and tried again. "Aunt Phyllis?"

Aunt Phyllis stilled, but didn't turn. "Yes, Ariane?"

"I . . . I want to apologize, Aunt Phyllis. For arguing with you. I didn't mean what I said. I know you love me, I know you love Mom, I just . . . it's been . . . it's been a rough few days."

Aunt Phyllis looked around at last. Her eyes glistened. "A rough few months, you mean," she said in a low voice. "I'm sorry too, Ariane. I never should have suggested your mother wouldn't be proud of you. I know she would. But Ariane, *fighting* . . ."

"I know." Ariane still didn't want to tell Aunt Phyllis *why* she had hit Shania. "I'm sorry. She said something that set me off, and I . . ."

Aunt Phyllis smiled a little. "You have the Forsythe

temper, that's all. I have it too. Which is why I lost it last night."

"Can you forgive me?"

"Will you forgive me?"

They had spoken at the same instant. Ariane and her aunt looked at each other and laughed.

"Come here." Aunt Phyllis opened her arms.

Ariane went to her, meeting her aunt's hug with one of her own. She closed her eyes and for a moment allowed herself to imagine she was hugging her mother again. *You're never too old to need a hug*, her mother had said to her once when Ariane was heartbroken over some stupid boy. She squeezed Aunt Phyllis a little tighter. That had been just before her mom disappeared.

They let go and smiled at each other shyly. "Am I still grounded?" Ariane asked hesitantly. "I know I deserve it, but it won't happen again . . ."

Aunt Phyllis's eyes narrowed, and Ariane thought she knew what was coming. But her aunt surprised her. "We'll call it a suspended sentence. Any more fighting this school year, and this grounding gets added to the one you deserve for the new incident. But stay out of trouble, and the sentence won't be carried out."

"Fair enough." Ariane took a huge breath, feeling as if a heavy weight had been lifted from her shoulders. "What's for breakfast? I'm starved!"

"Cold cereal, I'm afraid." Aunt Phyllis closed the dishwasher door. "And you'll have to fix it yourself. I'm due at a Friends of the Library meeting downtown in half an hour. Then some of us are going for lunch, and after that I've got a lot of errands to run—I probably won't be back until dinner time." She took her car keys from a hook by the door leading to the back porch. "Put your dishes in the dishwasher and run it when you're done breakfast, won't you, sweetie? And don't forget to clean your room! I'll see you later."

She grabbed her coat from a peg and stepped onto the back porch. Pendragon slipped inside as she opened the door. "Mrrrr?" he said, rubbing her ankle. "Mrrow!"

Aunt Phyllis scratched him behind the ears. "Too cold for you, old man?" she said. "Ariane, can you make sure he's got food? He went out first thing this morning—I don't think he's eaten yet."

"Will do," Ariane said. As if he understood, Pendragon came in and gave her ankles a quick polish in turn. She watched Aunt Phyllis go down the back walk and enter the garage. A moment later she heard her ancient Oldsmobile driving away.

Feeling much, much happier than when she'd run out of the house the previous evening, Ariane fed Pendragon, ate her Shreddies, drank a large glass of orange juice, and then ran upstairs to her room. She owed someone else an apology, too.

She had a Facebook account that she almost never used, and after all the crap she'd gone through at every school she'd attended in the past couple of years, she was too wary to leave her profile public. But she was willing to bet Wally had no such qualms. Ariane did a quick search and a moment later, his friendly, homely face was grinning at her from the screen.

She clicked Message, and typed:

I'm sorry I ran out like that. What happened when Felicia came home? Email or call, don't Facebook. Here's my email address and phone number. Whatever you do, don't let Flish get hold of them . . . although maybe I deserve it after leaving that mess in her room. I hope she didn't blame you . . .

She added her contact information, then got up from the computer.

She didn't even make it to the door before a bell-like tone announced new mail.

Wally probably lives at his computer on weekends, she thought, returning to her desk. She opened the message.

Thanks for nothing. When I said you could borrow Felicia's clothes, I didn't expect you to trash her room! OF COURSE she blamed me for it! She went postal on my butt. You're lucky I'm not a grease spot on the kitchen floor.

I don't know what she and her fellow hags were up to last night, but she came in wetter and muddier than you and I were, and with a big ugly bruise on her chest. She's lucky Mom and Dad weren't home or she'd be a grease spot on the kitchen floor.

Ariane didn't bother trying to suppress her smile of satisfaction.

We've got to talk. But don't call. Stick to email. I don't want Felicia to know anything about this.
Wally.

Ariane clicked REPLY. *I'm home.* She typed in her address. *Come see me. Call first.* She clicked SEND, then went to her bookshelf and pulled out an old children's book: *The Adventures of King Arthur and the Knights of the Round Table.* She lay back on her bed, intending to bone up some more on the legends she seemed to have become a part of somehow.

The sound of the doorbell playing the first six bars of "God Save the Queen" woke her. Something sharp was digging into her side. She had dozed off while reading and rolled over onto the book. She grimaced at the pain. Then, "God save our gracious Queen . . ." started up again, and she hopped to her feet and ran downstairs.

"Coming!" she shouted. Just to be safe, though, she looked out through the peephole in the door before she opened it.

Wally stood on the porch. He leaned in toward the peephole—which had a most alarming effect on her view of his face—gave her a lopsided grin, and said, "May I come in?"

Ariane unlocked the door and opened it wide. "Did you try to call?" she said as he stepped past her into the hall. "I didn't hear the phone . . ."

"I didn't call. I didn't want my *darling* sister to hear me talking to you." His grin turned into a frown. "I really did think she'd kill me when she saw what you'd done to her room. And I *really* thought she'd kill *you.* But when she came in last night, it looked like you'd gotten the better of her. So what happened? Give!"

"I'll tell you the whole story," Ariane promised. "Come into the living room and sit down. You want a drink?"

"Sure."

Ariane used the time it took to pull two Diet Cokes from the refrigerator to debate how much she would tell Wally. There were parts of it, mostly the parts where Felicia and her friends were trying to strip her in the parking lot, that she'd just as soon gloss over. Especially with a boy.

He doesn't need to know everything, she told herself as she took the Cokes into the living room. So as she started describing what had happened, she didn't intend to tell him much. Except . . .

. . . except, it felt so good to be able to talk to someone about it. Someone who had also seen the Lady of the Lake. Someone who wouldn't think she was crazy. Even if that someone was Wally. And so, in the end, she told him everything, even the embarrassing parts.

Besides, she told herself, *he's your partner in this quest thing. The Lady said so. And he's Felicia's sister. He needs to know what his sister is capable of . . . and what I'm capable of, too.*

Wally's eyes widened as he listened. "Wow," he said when she finished. "No wonder Flish looked like a wet cat— and was madder than one."

Ariane grinned.

"So you can make water . . . do things," Wally said. "That makes sense, I guess, if you're the Lady of the Lake. And at least if we ever do come face to face with Merlin, maybe you can save our butts." Wally gave her another of his lopsided grins. "But I still don't see how we're going to find the shards of Excalibur before a wizard does!"

Even with her new determination to carry out the Lady's quest, Ariane felt embarrassed to hear their goal stated so baldly. It sounded like bad dialogue from a straight-to-video sword-and-sorcery flick. "I'm not sure," she said. "Maybe the Lady would have told us, if she hadn't been pulled away so suddenly. But I've got an idea. When I . . . connected . . . with the lake, I could kind of sense everything in it. The fish, the rocks, even the trash. And the Lady said I would hear the . . . um, 'song of the sword.' So maybe if I try, I can figure out how to, you know, see . . . or feel . . . or whatever . . . the shards. Somehow." *I don't even know the right words to talk about magic!* "But I'm not sure how to start."

Wally looked thoughtful. "What you need is a séance."

Ariane blinked. "What, with spirits rapping on the window and levitating the table? Get real."

"I think we can do without the rapping spirits . . . although that would be a great name for a hip-hop group in Harry Potter's wizarding world . . ."

"Wally!"

"Sorry."

"Séances are for communicating with the dead. How is that going to help me? I don't want to talk to any dead people."

"Did I say anything about dead people?

"But a séance—"

"So don't call it a séance. Look, the way I understand it, the point of a séance, or a crystal ball, or any of that other psychic mumbo-jumbo, is to help you concentrate. Even though most of the 'mediums' . . ." He frowned. "Or should that be 'media'? Well, anyway—even though most people who do this stuff are frauds—"

"Most?"

"—that doesn't change the fact that sitting in the dark, holding hands, and concentrating on a candle is a great way to focus your mind. You—we—need to explore your power. There's just the two of us to do for Excalibur what all the king's horses and all the king's men couldn't do for Humpty Dumpty. We have to know what abilities you have. And we're definitely going to have to know where to look!"

"Even if we figure out where to look, I don't know how we're supposed to get there," Ariane said. "Unless you happen to have a private jet stashed away somewhere, we're pretty much stuck in Regina." She paused. "You don't, do you?"

Wally laughed. "Afraid not. Well, one thing at a time. What do you say? A séance? Tonight?"

"Why not now?"

"I think it will help if it's dark. And besides . . ." He blushed. "I have to be home by four to clean my room. Ms. Carson made me promise."

Ariane laughed.

"Hey, a promise is a promise!"

"I'm sorry, I'm not laughing at you." It was *almost* the truth. "I'm supposed to clean my room too. It's just—it's all so silly. We're on a quest to find a mystical sword and save the planet from the most powerful sorcerer of all time—but we can't get to it right now because we have to clean our rooms!"

Wally's scowl turned to a grin, then to a laugh. Ariane joined in, and in a moment both of them were laughing so hard that Ariane's laugh turned into the unfortunate snorting sound she'd never been able to control—and that just made them both laugh harder.

"Well, you two seem to be having a ball!" Aunt Phyllis's voice cut through their mirth. She was standing in the French doors that connected the hallway to the living room, holding a bag of groceries with both arms. "Who's your friend, Ariane?"

Aunt Phyllis's tone made it clear that Ariane was on shaky ground. She realized two things at the same time. First, Wally was a boy. And second, though her aunt and she had never discussed the rules about having boys over, Ariane was quite sure the rules would be strict. She hurried to make introductions before Aunt Phyllis got *entirely* the wrong idea. "Aunt Phyllis, this is Wally Knight. Wally, this is my Aunt Phyllis."

Wally stood up, wiped his hand on his jeans, and held it out to Aunt Phyllis. "Pleased to meet you. Oh . . . sorry." Apparently realizing belatedly she couldn't shake his hand while she was holding groceries, he awkwardly withdrew it again.

Ariane watched Aunt Phyllis's face, and felt relief when her aunt smiled. "Nice to meet you, Wally."

Struck by sudden inspiration, Ariane said, "Aunt Phyllis, can Wally come for dinner?" She really should have asked Wally first, but it made sense. "That way we can get started on our . . . um . . . homework project even sooner."

"You two are partners?"

Wally, after one startled glance at Ariane, caught on quickly. "Yeah," he said. "Partners."

"What kind of project is it?"

Oops. "It's . . . um, a kind of, uh, cross-grade, cross-curriculum thing. Younger students working with older ones. We're supposed to combine, um, history and, uh, English. We need to do some research. On my computer. On the Internet."

"Mine's broken," Wally put in.

"Oh. I see," Aunt Phyllis said, in a voice that made it clear she didn't—not entirely. She made her way into the living room, still holding her bag of groceries. "What are you researching?"

"King Arthur," Ariane said.

Aunt Phyllis stumbled. Ariane jumped to her feet in alarm, but her aunt had already caught herself. A can of tomatoes fell out of her bag and hit the carpet with a thump.

Wally picked it up and put it back into the bag. Aunt Phyllis hardly seemed to notice. She was staring at Ariane, her face so pale Ariane worried she might be getting sick. Ariane was about to say that maybe dinner wasn't such a good idea when Aunt Phyllis blinked a couple of times, then seemed to gather her wits. She looked at Wally and smiled, though it looked a little forced. "Thank you for picking that up, Wally. Honestly, sometimes I think I have two left feet." Her smile grew warmer and more sincere. "Now, about dinner. How does six-thirty sound?"

"That'll be perfect!" Wally said, with a grin. "I'd better go now and get started on my room. I'll see you for dinner, Ariane, Mrs. . . . ." He stopped, and blushed. (*He blushes at everything*, Ariane thought. *It's kind of sweet.*) "I'm sorry. I just realized I don't know your last name."

"It's Forsythe. The same as Ariane's. But it's not Mrs. I've never been married."

Wally didn't say anything, but Ariane felt she had to explain. "My mother didn't change her name when she got married. And since my father didn't stick around long enough to see me born, she wasn't about to give me *his* name."

"Oh." Wally obviously didn't know how to respond.

"Well. Uh, thank you, Mrs. . . . Ms . . . .Forsythe. For the dinner invitation. I'll see you at six-thirty." He gathered up his coat and went out, whistling the theme to *Star Wars*.

Aunt Phyllis gave Ariane another odd look. "Homework partners?"

Wally wasn't the only one who blushed easily. "Homework partners," Ariane said firmly. "That's all."

"Researching King Arthur." Aunt Phyllis's eyes moved away from Ariane to the mantelpiece. Ariane followed her gaze—and found herself looking at a photograph of her mother when she was only a little older than Ariane, laughing against the backdrop of a sunny lake.

"Yes." Ariane frowned. "Why?"

Aunt Phyllis didn't answer. She looked at the photograph for another moment, then turned away as if she hadn't heard. "I'd better put the groceries away." She disappeared into the kitchen.

Ariane got up from the couch and went to the mantle. She'd seen that photo of her mother all her life. Oddly, she never felt sad when looking at it. Maybe because it had been taken ten years before Ariane was born. Looking at it was almost like looking at a stranger . . . but a nice stranger, a girl Ariane felt she would have liked to have known.

The refrigerator door slammed in the kitchen, and then Ariane heard Aunt Phyllis say a most uncharacteristic swear word. A moment later she emerged into the hall, face flushed. "Would you believe I forgot to buy milk? Ariane, would you mind running up to the 7-Eleven?"

"Uh . . . sure." Ariane went into the front hall and pulled on her spare jacket, already missing her ruined leather one. She was more than a little surprised at her aunt's language.

Aunt Phyllis might have "the Forsythe temper," but she didn't actually seem angry. It was more like she was on edge. Ariane would've asked what was going on, but Aunt Phyllis had already returned to the kitchen.

Ariane unlocked the inner door, crossed the porch, and stepped through the outer door into the chilly air. She was glad to have the excuse to slip out for a few minutes, not only because she needed some fresh air and to stretch her legs, but because it would give Aunt Phyllis a chance to calm down.

Was it Wally? she wondered. *Maybe she's worried we're going to be more than friends . . . or already are. Though why would Aunt Phyllis care? You'd think she'd be happy if I found a boyfriend.*

Well, maybe. But I'm pretty sure she wouldn't want me to invite him to my bedroom.

She shook her head as she crossed the yard. As if there could be anything like that between her and Wally. He wasn't exactly handsome, he was scrawny, he was at least a year younger (and a head shorter) than she was, he was a geek, his sister was her mortal enemy, and . . .

. . . and it had felt really good to laugh with someone like that.

Not a chance, she told herself firmly. *Not . . . a . . . chance!*

She strode north along Wallace Street to College Avenue. As she jaywalked across the street, a car turned south behind her. On the north side of College, she glanced back, just in time to see the car make a U-turn halfway down Wallace and park in front of her house.

It was a white Ford Focus—just like the car she'd seen with the mysterious blue glow inside the night before. It was facing her, engine still running, lights on.

Ariane picked up speed, not exactly alarmed, but definitely weirded out. She walked a block west to Winnipeg Street, then turned north to walk the four blocks to Victoria Avenue and the 7-Eleven which did a brisk business selling junk food to the students from the two nearby high schools. Today, though, she ignored the racks of potato chips and candy bars and went straight for the refrigerators in the back. She bought a two-litre container of one-percent milk, and headed outside.

As she ran back across Victoria Avenue, she again saw a white Ford Focus, this time parked on Winnipeg Street half a block from the intersection, facing her. Its lights were off and there was no one inside that she could see, so she kept walking toward it. *There are lots of Ford Focuses.* She frowned. *Ford Foci?* That didn't sound right, either. She shook her head. *Anyway, this isn't necessarily the same one.* Still, as she reached it, she glanced at it as casually as she could.

What she saw made her stumble. It had a corporate logo on the door: gold letters in Old English script spelling out *ECS*.

Below the letters was the image of a golden sword.

She couldn't help looking over her shoulder every few steps all the way back to her house. The car stayed parked, and by the time she got home she'd managed to convince herself she was just being silly. It probably had nothing to do with her. She delivered the milk to Aunt Phyllis—who seemed to be her usual self again—then settled down in front of the TV for a couple of hours of mindless entertainment.

When Ariane saw that the movie channel was playing *Monty Python and the Holy Grail*, she sighed. *It figures,* she thought, pulling her legs up to sit cross-legged on the couch while she watched. *It figures.*

IT DIDN'T REALLY take Wally long to clean his room, because it wasn't very messy to begin with. (He knew he was unusually neat for a teenage boy. It kind of worried him.) At around five o'clock, with an hour and a half to kill before he was due back at Ariane's house for supper—Ms. Carson had raised no objection to his going; in fact, she seemed rather glad to be rid of him—he sat down at his computer to find out everything he could about King Arthur and his contemporaries.

An hour later, he'd had his fill of Arthur, Lancelot, Guinevere, The Lady of the Lake, Merlin, Mordred, Morgan le Fay, the Knights of the Round Table, the whole murderous, adulterous, incestuous, backstabbing lot of them. It wasn't that he couldn't find any information: he found thousands of pages of it. But it was all contradictory. There seemed to be a hundred different versions of every Arthurian legend—a thousand, if you counted all of the novels and plays and movies and TV shows and even *musicals*, for crying out loud, from *Camelot* to *Spamalot*—and nobody had anything definitive to offer on what had really happened. Or even *if* it had really happened. Those who believed Arthur had existed thought he was some kind of British war leader who managed to stave off the ongoing Saxon invasion of England for a few years, within a century or two after the departure of the Roman legions. Merlin might have been some sort of shaman—or might not have existed at all. And the Lady of

the Lake was either some kind of pagan priestess, or as myth-
ical as Merlin.

Except he'd actually *met* the Lady of the Lake . . .

. . . or someone *claiming* to be the Lady.

He frowned, wondering why the thought hadn't
occurred to him before. Just because she *said* she was the
Lady didn't mean she *was*. And just because she said that
Merlin was evil and they had to stop him didn't make those
statements true, either. After all, in most versions of the
legend Merlin was a good guy and it was the *Lady* who was
shifty and unreliable, pursuing her own hidden agenda.

The clock at the bottom right corner of his screen flicked
to 6:04. Wally, who was pretty sure his sister searched his
room regularly in search of blackmail material, cleared his
browser history and re-opened his home page, a news site.
He bent over to pick up his runners, which he had kicked off
under the desk when he sat down. He glanced over the head-
lines as he put on his shoes. *Suicide Bomber Kills 12 . . . Civil
War Looms in Famine-Plagued Country . . . Terrorist Threat
Considered High . . . Habitat Loss Threatens Endangered
Species . . .*

Wally wasn't very interested in politics, but he'd heard his
parents arguing about it often enough. His mother supported
one party, his father another, and over the course of his short life
both parties had been in power. But the one thing he'd taken
away from his parents' arguments was that no matter who was
running things, no matter how big the majority, the government
could never get everything done that needed to be done. His
mother wanted fines for polluting companies, his father wanted
a reduction in the size of the civil service, and both of them hated
the fact that the prime minister couldn't simply issue decrees

and make things happen, but instead had to deal and cajole, "caving in to special interests!" as his mother put it or, in his father's words, "bribing the public with their own tax money!"

Maybe the whole world would be better off with one strong leader in charge, he thought as he pushed his chair away from the desk and headed out the door. *Someone who actually knows what he's doing. Just like England was better off under King Arthur.*

Twenty minutes later, he stepped through the open outer door into the porch of Ariane's house, and rang the doorbell. "I'll get it!" he heard Ariane shout, and a moment later the front door swung open. "Come in!" she said, stepping aside to let him enter.

As he did so, a savoury smell set his mouth watering. "Mmmmm. Something smells *good.*"

"Mustard-smeared protein," Ariane said.

"Huh?"

Ariane laughed. "That's what Mom used to call it. Smear any kind of meat or fish with mustard, sprinkle on a few herbs, stick it in the oven. Works every time."

Wally smacked his lips. "Yum! And tonight's protein is . . .?"

"Pork tenderloin," said Aunt Phyllis, coming to the door of the kitchen. "And it's almost ready. Ariane, could you set the table?"

"I'll help," said Wally, earning a surprised glance from Ariane.

A few minutes later, they were seated before a feast of "mustard-smeared protein," peas, rice, and salad.

"Your mother didn't mind you missing dinner?" Aunt

Phyllis asked, pouring teriyaki sauce on her rice. She handed the bottle to Wally.

When in Rome, he thought, and anointed his rice likewise. "My parents are both away right now. Ms. Carson, our housekeeper, is fixing our meals and sleeping over. And the way Flish and I have been at each other's throats lately, I think Ms. Carson was relieved I was going out." Wally handed the teriyaki sauce to Ariane, then looked back to catch Aunt Phyllis's bemused face. "Um, I probably shouldn't have said that . . ."

"Never mind, dear." Aunt Phyllis delicately cut a slice off her pork. "And Flish is . . .?" She popped the pork into her mouth.

"My sister. Felicia." Wally took a bite of teriyaki-laced rice. *Not bad! Not bad at all.*

"Younger?"

"Older. By almost four years."

Aunt Phyllis nodded sympathetically. "That's an awkward difference in age during the teenage years. But don't worry, I'm sure you'll be best friends when you're a few years older."

"Maybe," Wally said. *Sure. And the Devil will be hosting skating parties in hell.* "Maybe."

Ariane, thinking about what she and Wally planned to attempt after dinner, hardly heard the small talk. But she refocused in a hurry when Aunt Phyllis asked, "So you and Ariane are working on a project on King Arthur?"

Ariane glanced sharply at Wally. His face gave nothing away. "Looks that way."

"Even though you're in different grades?" Aunt Phyllis took a bite of peas.

Ariane decided to jump in. "It's a sort of . . . mentoring program. To foster school spirit. Get the kids in different grades to know each other. That kind of thing." *You're babbling . . .*

"How unusual." Aunt Phyllis sipped from her water glass. "But why King Arthur?"

"He's just interesting," Ariane said. "Camelot, Guinevere, Merlin, all that stuff. Knights in shining armour. It just sounded way better than, like, researching coal mining in Wales or something."

"Not to me," Aunt Phyllis said. "King Arthur is a myth. And a pretty silly one. Magical swords. Round tables. I'd think you'd find it awfully childish."

Ariane gave her aunt a surprised look. Aunt Phyllis almost sounded annoyed again, like she had before she'd sent Ariane out for the milk.

"Aren't you both a little old to be wasting your time on fairy tales?" Aunt Phyllis continued, lifting another forkful of rice.

"We're not *that* old," Wally put in. Ariane saw him looking anxiously from her to her aunt, as though he could sense the building tension. "Weren't you ever interested in King Arthur, Ms. Forsythe?"

"When I was a child," Aunt Phyllis said "But I grew out of it." She smiled at Wally, or at least tried to. It wasn't very convincing. "Don't mind me, Wally. Of course you can do your report on whatever you like. King Arthur just . . . wouldn't be my choice."

Ariane frowned. It felt like Aunt Phyllis was hiding something. *Something about Mom. Something about King Arthur. The Lady said Mom refused her power. Does Aunt Phyllis actually* know *about that?* She was dying to ask. But if *Ariane* asked too many questions, Aunt Phyllis might start asking questions that *she* didn't want to answer.

So she dropped the subject, and Wally followed her lead. The rest of the meal passed without a mention of King Arthur. Instead, Ariane found herself learning a lot more about the social dynamics of the school fencing team than she felt she really needed to.

Knowing what they were planning to attempt, she began to chafe at the delay as time ticked by and the small talk continued. Wally didn't seem to share her anxiety: he helped himself to seconds, and then to thirds. Simultaneously amused and frustrated, Ariane wondered how a boy his size could eat so much.

Eventually even Wally was finished. But then they had to clear away the dishes. Wally, who had astonished Ariane when he helped set the table, astonished her again by offering to help load the dishwasher.

Finally, Aunt Phyllis let them go upstairs. "You two go work on your project now. I'll look in a little bit later with some cocoa and sweets."

And to make sure we're not fooling around, I'll bet, Ariane thought. But there was no point in stating the obvious or fighting the inevitable—though she hoped their "séance" would be over before Aunt Phyllis knocked . . . *if* she knocked.

Two minutes later she and Wally were in her room and free to talk. "Do you think your Aunt Phyllis knows?" Wally said, his eyes wide. "That your mom met the Lady of the Lake? That's wild."

"I don't know," Ariane said. It was hard to imagine, Aunt Phyllis believing in the Lady. Short of asking her outright, she didn't know of any way to find out, either. "Anyway, never mind that. Let's get on with the . . . thing."

"The séance?" Wally laughed and held up his hands when he saw her expression. "Sorry! How about . . . um . . . 'meditation ritual'? Or maybe . . . 'self-hypnosis session'?"

Ariane snorted. "Not much better. How do you know so much about them, anyway? Don't tell me you're a medium."

"More like an extra-small." He spread his arms and looked down at his scrawny body, and Ariane laughed. He looked up again, grinning. "I read a lot, that's all. And, uh . . ." He reddened a little. "And I saw Flish try it once. With her gang. Which is why I like to call them the coven."

"You saw her? She let you watch?"

"Not exactly. But I overheard what they were planning as they went into her room. So I spied on them. Through the keyhole. See, uh, witches, when they do magic, sometimes they, uh . . ." His voice trailed off.

Ariane remembered something *she'd* read about witches. "Don't tell me they were naked!"

"No . . ." Wally sounded a little wistful, and must have realized it, because he turned even redder. "No. But they stripped down to their underwear." Now he was so red Ariane thought he might spontaneously combust. "I mean, I've seen Flish in her underwear before, no big deal, but

Shania is . . . I mean . . . look, just forget it, OK? The point is, I kind of know how it works."

Ariane felt a pang of . . . though she hated to admit it . . . jealousy. When Mr. Stanton had broken up her fight with Shania, his eyes had been all over the other girl. He'd hardly glanced at Ariane until he took her to the office. And now Wally, too? *Boys!* She grimaced. "Sorry I asked. Let's get on with it."

Wally nodded. He'd brought a backpack with him. He opened it and took out a candle. It was fat, round, and white, about ten centimetres in diameter and twenty centimetres tall. Ornate silver lettering wound its way around the candle's circumference. It looked perfectly suited to an arcane ritual—until Ariane picked it up to get a better look. "Happy New Year 1998?"

Wally shrugged. "It was all I could find."

Ariane laughed. "So where should we put it?"

"Somewhere we can't accidentally set fire to the place?"

Ariane looked around. The only good-sized bit of open floor in her room was at the foot of her bed, where a round pink throw rug covered the oak floorboards. "Help me move the rug."

Together they rolled it up and shoved it under the bed. Then Wally put the candle on the floor, took a book of matches from his pocket, and lit the wick. "Turn off the light," he said.

Ariane clicked off the switch while Wally settled himself cross-legged on one side of the candle. Now the only illumination came from the blue-green glow of the computer's aquarium screen saver and the candle's yellow flame, flickering in the slight draft from under the door.

Ariane pointed to the monitor. "Should I turn that off?"

"No, leave it on. If the candle doesn't work, you can always try concentrating on the virtual fish." He grinned. "Come to think of it, that might be more appropriate for the Lady of the Lake."

"Don't call me that!"

"Princess of the Pond? Maiden of the Mud? Miss Teen Watersprite of Twenty . . . OK, OK, I'll shut up." Her phaser-like glare had finally penetrated his shields of obliviousness. He indicated the floor on the opposite side of the candle from him. "Come on, let's give this a try."

"We don't have to take off our clothes, do we?" Ariane said innocently, folding her legs under her.

"Very funny," Wally muttered, blushing again, and Ariane grinned. But her grin faded as the strangeness of what they were attempting sank in. She looked around uneasily. The wavering flame made shadows dance in the corners, giving Ariane the unnerving feeling that strange, living *things* slithered, skulked, and skittered just on the edge of her vision.

Too much imagination . . .

"What do we do now?"

"First, hold hands." Wally held out his, and Ariane took them. They were warm and dry and not unpleasant to touch. Thanks to Aunt Phyllis, the thought crossed her mind that this whole thing might just be a scheme of Wally's to hold hands with a girl, but she shoved the notion aside.

"Now what?"

"Stare at the candle, and concentrate on . . . whatever it is you have inside you. This 'power' you feel. Don't look away." Ariane focused on the leaping flame while he continued to murmur. "Watch the flame. Reach out for the power. It's there inside you. Look for it. Reach for it. Watch the flame . . ."

The candle flame swelled to fill her vision, and Wally's voice seemed to fade into the distance. She looked past the glowing corona of hot gas into the darker, cooler centre. It looked almost like a tunnel, like a doorway . . . a passageway to something else, some new level of concentration . . .

. . . some new level of power, some new facet of the Lady's gift . . .

The dark centre of the candle flame rushed toward her—swallowed her. But in that darkness, she heard a song. Not the song of the water this time, but something different, harsher, colder, and harder . . .

And then light, as bright and white as lightning, banished the darkness and cast everything into sharp relief. Ariane and Wally jerked apart and stared at her desk. The light was blazing from the computer monitor. As they watched, it darkened and turned a deep blue. Something swirled in the centre of it, coalesced, and became an image of a bloodstained sword—gripped by a mailed fist.

A voice boomed from the speakers, deep and powerful enough to rattle the window. "The sword is not for you. Abandon your quest, or face the wrath of Merlin!"

Wally's grip on her hand tightened. Ariane felt grateful for the human contact.

"Merlin grants you this warning because he is merciful. But his mercy is not unlimited. Do not expect it again!"

The image of the sword vanished. The blue changed to the blazing white light that had startled them a few moments ago. Wincing, Ariane threw her hand across her eyes. And then the light was gone, and the monitor once again showed computerized fish swimming in a virtual aquarium. In the sudden hush, Ariane heard the sound of a car starting up outside. She leaped to her feet, knocking over the candle, which splattered hot wax across the floor before sputtering out. "Watch it!" Wally cried, but Ariane hardly heard him. She raced to the window, jerked up the blinds, and peered out into the night just in time to see a car pulling away from the curb . . . a white Ford Focus.

Wally joined her. "Who was that?"

"Someone who was trying to scare us." *And succeeding.*

"But . . . how?" Wally walked over to the computer. "How could he . . . reach inside your computer like that?" He sounded tense . . . even frightened, though Ariane doubted he'd ever admit that to her. "I've never seen a monitor light up like that before. Something would have to be short-circuiting and arcing inside . . . but the thing is still working. Nice trick." He managed a smile. "And it sounded like he got James Earl Jones to deliver his lines. Mr. Darth Vader himself." The smile faded. "Do you think he was spying on us? Was that *Merlin* outside your house?"

"I don't know," she said. "But whether that was him, or someone who works for him . . . he knows who I am now." She felt a chill. "And where I live. I've seen that same car several times. It was parked on Winnipeg Street this afternoon. I walked right by it. It even had a sword on the door. If it belongs to Merlin, he's practically advertising."

Wally looked up sharply. "What?"

"Not a real sword. A picture of a sword. And some letters. ECS."

Wally's mouth fell open. "Oh, wow. *Wow.*"

Ariane stared at him, irritated. "Wow *what*?"

"ECS. It stands for Excalibur Computer Systems. Rex Major's company."

"Rex who?"

"Rex Major!" Wally said. "He's like . . . Bill Gates and Steve Jobs, all rolled into one. One of the richest men in the world. His Excalibur server software is everywhere. The whole Internet practically runs on it." He gasped. "My phone—remember the way it lit up in the underwater chamber? Just like this computer. It was a smartphone—connected to the Internet." He leaned forward, excited. "If Merlin is still alive, he wouldn't be calling himself Merlin anymore, would he? He'd have to have a disguise, become someone else—something other than a wizard. *What if Rex Major is Merlin?* What if he's combined his magic with his computer software? He could extend his power anywhere the Internet reaches. And that's almost everywhere." His eyes widened. "And his name!"

"Rex Major?"

"It means High King in Latin!"

"But Merlin's not a king."

"But if the Lady was telling us the truth, he wants to be one. That's why he wants Excalibur—to take over the world." He looked at the window. "Rex Major wouldn't have been out there in person. But he's got offices everywhere. That must be one of his . . ." he grinned suddenly, as if he couldn't believe he was actually getting to use the word, ". . . minions."

Ariane felt a chill. "But . . . how are we supposed to beat someone like *that*?"

"The Lady said you could do it. With the power she gave

you." He looked down and nudged the fallen candle with his foot. "So do we try again?"

Ariane thought about it, recalling what had happened the first time they'd tried it, and suddenly she realized something: the strange new song she had heard in the mystical darkness still echoed in her mind. She shook her head. "No need," she said in wonder. "It worked."

"Really?"

"Really." Ariane spread her hands. "I can hear the song of the sword. I know where to find the first shard of Excalibur."

6

GOING WITH THE FLOW

Wally stared at Ariane. He opened his mouth to speak, not sure if he should ask "How?" or "Where?" first. Before he could make up his mind, the bedroom door opened and Aunt Phyllis stuck in her head.

Good thing I just turned on the lights, he thought. The fallen candle was just beside his foot; he nudged it under the bed. He couldn't do anything about the rug having been rolled up, but though Aunt Phyllis's eyes flickered over it, she didn't say anything about it. Instead, she smiled.

"Hello, you two! I've got some cookies and hot chocolate waiting downstairs for dessert, if you're ready."

Wally looked at Ariane. *Are we?*

"That would be great, Aunt Phyllis," Ariane said. "Perfect timing."

"How is the project coming?" Aunt Phyllis asked as they followed her down the stairs.

"We've made a good start," Ariane said.

"I thought I heard a loud voice upstairs—a man's voice," Aunt Phyllis continued as she led them into the kitchen. "Gave me a start, until I figured out it must have been coming from your computer."

Ariane looked at Wally.

"It was a YouTube clip," he answered without hesitation. "Of this cheesy King Arthur movie. The volume was set too high. I'm sorry if it startled you."

"Oh, that's all right. Now, you two sit at the table . . ."

In two minutes she had poured three big mugs of hot chocolate and Wally was biting into a thick chocolate-chunk macaroon. He thought he'd died and gone to heaven. *Why can't Ms. Carson bake like this?* "You're a terrific cook, Ms. Forsythe."

"Thank you," said Aunt Phyllis. "Please, have another."

Wally obeyed, happily. Ariane didn't say anything: her mouth was already full with *her* second cookie. She polished it off and started on a third. "Hungry?" he asked.

"Famished," she replied, chewing more slowly.

Aunt Phyllis nibbled daintily on her first cookie. "So, Wally. You said at dinner you grew up in Regina. Has your family lived here a long time?"

Wally nodded. *At least this is safer ground than strange voices in the bedroom.* "My parents were born and raised here too, and my grandparents on my father's side. My father's father's parents moved here around 1915 from Cannington Manor."

Aunt Phyllis nodded. The name clearly meant something to her. Just as clearly, Ariane had never heard of it. "Where's that?" she asked. She finished her third cookie, but though she was eyeing the plate, didn't pick up a fourth.

"Thirty-five kilometres or so southwest of Moosomin, not far from Moose Mountain Provincial Park. A bunch of English people settled it in the late 1800s. They thought they could recreate a proper Victorian English farming village on the prairie. It boomed for a while, but that was before Canadian Pacific decided not to build a rail line to the town. The nearest branch line ended up ten miles south, and that was pretty much the end of Cannington Manor. There's hardly anything there now."

"Well, there's a very interesting interpretative centre," Aunt Phyllis said. "I've been there. It's a provincial heritage site. Were your great-grandparents English, then?"

"Great-grandfather Knight was. He was the youngest of five boys, so there wasn't much of an inheritance for him to look forward to in England. He came to Cannington Manor as a teenager because he'd seen one of the ads Captain Edward Pierce had put in the London newspapers."

"Ah," Aunt Phyllis said. "Your great-grandfather was one of the infamous 'bachelors.'"

Wally grinned. "That's right. And apparently a pretty wild one too."

Ariane gave her aunt and Wally a bewildered look. "What are you guys talking about?"

Aunt Phyllis sipped her hot chocolate. "Captain Pierce—who may or may not have been a real captain—planned to set up an agricultural school where young men from England could learn to be Saskatchewan farmers. What he mostly ended up with were dissolute young men more interested in drinking and carousing than farming."

"They hung out at Didsbury, this big estate run by the Beckton Brothers," Wally said. He'd read everything he could about Cannington Manor once he'd learned about the Knight family's connection to it. "Ernest, Billie, and Bernie Beckton had inherited quite a bit of money back in England, and it went a long way out here on the frontier. They bred thoroughbreds—horses—and raced them too, as far away as Chicago. They even hunted foxes, you know, red coats, hounds, the whole bit. And they were famous for the parties they held at their lakeside cabin."

"But eventually, like everyone else, even they gave up and left for greener pastures," Aunt Phyllis continued when Wally stopped to take another sip of his hot chocolate. "Got married and took their wives back to England, I think. A lot of the 'bachelors' drifted farther west. A few headed up to the Yukon, prospecting for gold. Others enlisted in the British army and fought in the Boer War. Your great-grandfather must have been one of the few who stayed."

Wally nodded. "He met and married my great-grandmother. She'd moved here from Germany with her parents. And despite all the partying, he apparently did learn a little bit about farming—enough to make a go of a homestead. But when the town started to dry up and blow away, he decided he wanted his family to have more opportunities than he'd had, so he moved to Regina and started a real-estate company."

Ariane's Aunt Phyllis's eyes widened. "You mean, you're *the* Knights? As in Knight Real Estate and Development? As in the Knight Towers downtown?"

"That's us," Wally said, a little uncomfortable. He didn't like to think about how his family had more money than anyone else he knew. It was his parents' money, not his. And as far as he was concerned, the only reason they had it was because they were never home.

Flish, on the other hand, judging by her shopping habits, had no problem at all enjoying the family wealth. And he no longer knew how she felt about their parents—not since she'd given up talking to him in favour of pushing him around.

Maybe he ought to change the subject after all. "May I have another cookie?"

"Help yourself." Aunt Phyllis pushed the plate in his direction. "Well, I must say, your great-grandfather sounds like quite a character."

"He was," Wally said. "He never saw himself as Canadian—'I was born an Englishman, I'll die an Englishman!' he used to say. Or that's what Grandma told me, anyway. But he never went back, even to visit. He used to tell Grandma it was 'too dangerous' for him to visit England again."

"Well, a lot of those 'bachelors' *were* the black sheep of the family," Aunt Phyllis said. "He probably committed some youthful indiscretion."

"I don't know," Wally said. He hadn't really thought about Grandma's stories for years. "There was something else he told Grandma, something about a treasure—"

He broke off, ancient family history suddenly driven from his mind. A newspaper lay on the far end of the table, open to the financial page. It was upside down from his vantage point, or he probably would have noticed the headline sooner:

REX MAJOR TO VISIT THUNDERHILL MINE

And, in smaller type underneath:

Server king planning diamond play?

"Wally, are you all right?" Aunt Phyllis asked.

Wally hardly heard her. He stared wide-eyed at Ariane and pointed mutely at the paper. She frowned at him, turned and looked—then grabbed the paper so suddenly she almost knocked her hot chocolate over.

"Ariane!" Aunt Phyllis snapped.

"Sorry, Aunt Phyllis. I just . . . um . . . this is something we could use for our project." Ariane plopped the paper down between her and Wally, and they scanned it together.

TORONTO (Staff) - Rex Major, president of Excalibur Computer Systems, has scheduled a visit to the Thunderhill Diamonds mine in the Northwest Territories for this weekend, the Financial Post learned yesterday. News of the trip has sparked speculation that Rex Major Industries (RMI) may be planning to invest in Thunderhill Diamonds, Inc., which owns and operates the mine.

Even though representatives of RMI insisted that the visit will be "strictly personal," stock prices for Thunderhill have risen sharply since yesterday.

"Mr. Major has long had an interest in the Canadian diamond mining industry, and decided to see for himself how the gems are extracted," said Thomas Horton, RMI's Director of Communications. "Nothing more should be read into it." Horton emphasized that Major will be making the visit alone, with no support staff.

Some financial analysts, however, were not convinced

by the company's disclaimer. "Rex Major doesn't do anything for purely personal reasons," said . . .

Ariane got to her feet. "We should get back to work."

"Huh? Uh, I mean, yeah, right, we should." Wally turned to Aunt Phyllis. "Thank you for the cookies and cocoa, Ms. Forsythe." He pushed his chair away from the table and stood. "They were delicious."

Aunt Phyllis looked at the newspaper, raised an eyebrow, then looked from Wally to Ariane and back again. "Was it something I said?"

"Of course not, Aunt Phyllis," Ariane said. "But we *are* trying to get this assignment done and I, uh, just had an idea." She picked up the paper. "May I take this?"

"Of course." Aunt Phyllis shook her head. "Although how you're going to work the *Financial Post* into a presentation on King Arthur—for English class, wasn't it?—I can't quite imagine." She smiled at Wally, who was looking at the plate of cookies with regret. "We can have more cookies and cocoa later, before Wally goes home, if you like."

Wally brightened. "Great! Uh, I mean, thanks!"

Ariane gave Aunt Phyllis a smile that belonged in a toothpaste commercial. "Back to work!" She ran up the stairs two steps at a time. Wally followed her, but not before giving Aunt Phyllis a sheepish grin.

When they were safely upstairs again, Ariane tossed the newspaper onto her bed. Wally pointed at it. "Does that mean what I think it does?"

Ariane nodded, her face flushed with excitement. "I think so. When I said I know where the first shard of Excalibur is, I meant I know in a kind of general way. When we did the, um, 'meditation ritual,' I could hear it singing in my mind, and I could sort of tell where it was coming from. North. A long, long way north. I figured if we went north . . . somehow . . . maybe as we got closer I could pin it down more precisely. But maybe we just got a break. If Rex Major really is Merlin—"

"I'm sure he is," Wally said.

"Well, *if* he is, and out of the blue he's suddenly decided to visit a diamond mine in the Northwest Territories, all by himself, then . . ."

"You figure the shard is at the mine."

"Or close by."

Wally nodded. "Okay. Which brings us to the next question." He stabbed at the picture of the Thunderhill Diamond Mine with his finger. "How do we get there?"

A long pause, while Ariane chewed on her lower lip. Finally, she said, "I've . . . got an idea."

Wally raised an eyebrow. "You don't sound convinced it's a *good* idea."

"I'm not. I . . . I need to think about it some more."

"So think out loud. But think fast, because Rex Major—Merlin—is headed there—," he pointed at the picture of the mine again, "—this weekend. Which is, like, *now*."

Ariane shook her head. "I don't want to say more until I know it'll work." Wally opened his mouth to protest, but Ariane plunged ahead. "No, Wally. I need to try this on my own."

Wally took a deep breath. "All right. You're the Lady—"

"Don't call me that!"

"—the one with the power, then. Is that better?"

From the look Ariane gave him, it wasn't.

"But we're supposed to be in this together, don't forget." *Or are we, really?* he wondered. The Lady had only *intended* to enlist Ariane. He'd been an afterthought, someone who had just happened by at the right—or maybe wrong—time. If this was the Fellowship of the Sword, he might be more Bill the Pony than Samwise Gamgee.

"If it works, I'll tell you right away." Ariane *sounded* as if she meant it.

"So what do we do for the rest of the evening? I can't leave if we're supposed to be working on some giant school project."

"We need to learn everything we can about Rex Major." Ariane indicated the computer. "How are you at Googling?"

Wally grinned, stretched out his arms and cracked his knuckles. "Try me!" But just as he was about to start typing, he stopped. "What about the warning?"

Ariane went over the window and peered out through the blinds. The street was deserted. "Nobody parked outside," she said. "I think we're safe."

Wally still hesitated. "Well," he said at last, "I suppose when you come right down to it, all he did was light up the monitor like a searchlight and throw Darth Vader's voice at us. And it's just a computer, isn't it? It's not like he can make it blow up." He shrugged, and started typing.

Nothing strange or magical happened, and within minutes, they were scanning through a list of hundreds of websites, news stories and magazine articles about Rex Major. But despite the apparent wealth of information, precise biographical details were scarce.

Rex Major had been born in England, but no one knew when he'd come to North America. He hadn't invented the

Excalibur software, but he had seen its potential and bought the original version from its creator, a man named Charles Wyndham. No one could understand why Wyndham had sold it outright for such a piddling sum: he'd never explained and died soon afterward. (Wally exchanged an alarmed glance with Ariane when they read that.)

Major lived in Toronto. He wasn't married, and he had no living relatives. He seemed completely focused on business—the analyst who had said "Rex Major doesn't do anything for personal reasons" hadn't been exaggerating—but he was also very generous and gave to numerous charities. He donated to all political parties equally; his own political convictions, if any, were a mystery. The only public comments he made concerned the activities of his company.

He was, in short, nothing more than a PR image. After almost an hour of digging, Wally shoved the mouse away in disgust. "He's hiding himself in plain sight. Which makes me even surer we're right. It's just what you'd expect from a wizard. But it doesn't help us."

Ariane was sitting on the edge of the bed with her head in her hands, looking gloomy. "He has unlimited resources, he's focused and ruthless, and if he's Merlin, then he has his own magic—which he may be able to piggyback on the Internet, so it's just about everywhere. And the only thing stopping him from taking over the world is . . . us?"

"He doesn't stand a chance," Wally said with a straight face.

Ariane stared at him for a moment, then burst out laughing. Wally joined in. Aunt Phyllis chose that moment to stick her head in again. "All done?"

Ariane grinned. "Checking up on us, Aunt Phyllis?"

Wally felt himself blushing, an annoyingly familiar sensation.

"I don't know what you mean," Aunt Phyllis said primly.

Ariane chuckled. "It's all right. Wally was just going home."

Wally blinked. "I was?"

Ariane gave him a dirty look.

"Oh. Right. I was." He stood up. "So, um, you'll tell me how that . . .thing . . . works out?"

"As soon as I can try it."

"Try what?" said Aunt Phyllis.

"Something on the computer," Ariane said.

"Ms. Forsythe?" said Wally. *Time to change the subject.*

"Yes, Wally?"

"May I have just one more chocolate chip cookie, to go?"

Aunt Phyllis laughed. "Of course, Wally."

A few minutes later Wally was on his way, one half-eaten cookie in his right hand, a second in a plastic baggie in his left. He stopped by the leaning gnome beneath the spruce and looked back up at Ariane's room. *Just what is she going to try?*

The light went out in her bedroom, and came on behind the tiny bathroom window next to it.

Whatever it is, I hope she's careful.

Munching his cookie, he headed home.

As soon as the door closed behind Wally, Ariane turned to head upstairs. Before she climbed the first step, though, Aunt Phyllis said, "Did you learn a lot about King Arthur?"

"Some," Ariane said. "We've still got work to do."

"So you'll be seeing more of Wally?" Aunt Phyllis sounded as if she was trying a little too hard to be casual. Ariane kept her own face as bland as she could.

"I guess so." She put her foot on the stairs. "I think I'll take a shower, then go to bed."

After a moment of silence, as though weighing her next words carefully, Aunt Phyllis sighed and said, "All right, dear."

Feeling a bit like she'd dodged an arrow, Ariane climbed to the second floor. She reached into her bedroom to turn off the light, then went into the bathroom, locked the door, and started the shower, adjusting the water until it had a nice, pleasant warmth. She stared at herself in the mirror. She didn't look like a powerful sorceress.

She widened her eyes and bared her teeth in a horrible grimace.

She still didn't.

But she couldn't deny what she had done to Felicia and friends. She couldn't deny that she had seen and spoken to the Lady of the Lake, a figure that existed only in myth—or so everyone thought. She couldn't deny that someone in a white Ford Focus was stalking her. She couldn't deny that someone calling himself Merlin had sent her a warning, telling her not to meddle in his business.

But most of all, she couldn't deny the song of the sword, humming away in the back of her head. The first shard of Excalibur pulled at her as though it were a magnet and she a compass needle. She wanted that shard, wanted to hold it, wanted to hear its full-throated song filling her mind instead of the faint, faint echo that was all she could hear now. That song excited her in a way she couldn't describe, even to herself, and certainly not to Wally. She had accepted the Lady's power in the hope it might help her find her mother, and that was still her hope: but now that the power was hers, she had to have the shard for its own sake. She could no more turn away from the quest she had been given than she could stop breathing.

That shard of Excalibur belonged to *her*, not to Merlin—and she intended to claim it.

And she was certain that the power the Lady had bequeathed could get her to the Thunderhill Diamond Mine . . .

. . . *if* she could figure out how to use it.

While talking to Wally she had remembered how she had felt in his kitchen, how it had seemed the water would have taken her with it down the drain, if only she had let it. And that had been *before* she had fully accepted the Lady's power. Now she not only intended to let it take her, she intended to *insist* that it take her.

She stared at her rather pale-looking face in the mirror, wished it good luck, then turned to the shower and stuck her hands into the spray.

The power inside her blossomed like a flower at the water's touch, revealing colours she had never seen before and crevices she longed to explore.

But for now there was just one part of that flower she wanted to examine. She closed her eyes to concentrate on the feel of the liquid on her skin. Just as she had in Wally's kitchen, she felt it flowing away from her, into the pipes, then into the sewer, off into the distance. She let her mind follow it, but it would only go so far before something held it back.

Oh, of course! My body. I can't leave it behind . . .

So she took it with her.

Suddenly she was rushing through the pipes at tremendous speed, following the water, not exactly seeing where it went—what was there to see inside a pitch-black sewer pipe? —but feeling the shape of the pipes it flowed through, feeling the water's unfocused frustration at being constrained. It wanted, in some elemental fashion, to be free, free of pipes and holding tanks and filters and grates, free to caress mud and sand and rock and ice, fish and fowl and weed and whale, to splash or crash against the shore, to form clouds in the sky and fall to the earth as rain. Whatever constraints humankind might place on it, water always found a path back into the natural world, seeping, splashing, puddling . . . and everywhere it went, she could go too she realized—and did, in a rush that would have been breathtaking if she had still been breathing. For a moment she felt confused and lost, her mind a whirl of wave and foam, black depths and sunlit shallows . . .

But though her body had dissolved, her mind and spirit remained intact. All the water in the world couldn't extinguish the spark of her soul unless she allowed it, and she would not allow it (*not this time*, something inside her whispered, and she felt a pang of fear), and so she centred her consciousness on a large expanse of water and willed her body back into existence.

She found herself in blackness, floundering. Her clothes pulled her down, but she reached the bottom quickly and kicked up again. Her head burst above the surface, and she gasped for air beneath a sky ablaze with stars. Treading water, she saw the black shapes of bushes and trees to her right. A few strong kicks put her in water shallow enough that she could stand up, and she splashed ashore, then turned to stare across the lake. The water had seemed warm when she had willed herself back into existence within it, but now that she had left it behind, cold gripped her. She remembered the trick she had pulled off in Wally's shower and ordered the water off of her. That helped, but it was still a cold night, even when she wasn't soaking wet, and she had already gotten chilled. She wrapped her arms tightly around her shivering body, teeth chattering.

She had no idea where she was, and the only lights she could see were so far away on the prairie horizon she might die of hypothermia before she could walk to them. There was nothing for it but to plunge back into the water and try to reverse whatever it was she had done that had brought her here, but she hesitated, remembering that tiny, chilling voice, her voice, whispering, *not this time . . .*

I could simply dissolve into water and vanish, she thought. *I could.*

The thought held her motionless (except for the shivering she couldn't control) for a long moment—not because she thought it could happen unless she let it, but out of perverse fascination. It would be simple, painless, clean . . . to everyone else it would seem she had just vanished, like her mother before her.

Like my mother . . .

The thought that her mother might have dissolved into water horrified her. *No,* she thought. *She rejected the power. She couldn't have . . .*

Could she? Even before I completely accepted the power, I had some of it. Could she have had enough to . . .?

She would have to think about it later. When she was warmer.

Putting aside her fear, she plunged back into the lake. The cold made her breath catch in her throat for a moment, but the instant she touched the power inside her, the water welcomed her and the chill disappeared. She dissolved into the swirling chaotic maelstrom, the water that could take her almost anywhere, because it was all connected, like the World Wide Web but with an even greater reach.

For now, though, there was only one place she wanted to go: home.

Unerringly, the power took her there, but then she was confronted with a new and terrifying problem: she could flow through her own bathroom, one with the spray in the still-running shower, but she couldn't materialize there. Again and again she tried, looping through sewer and lake and filtration plant and pipe, but her body would not take shape. Worse, she could feel herself tiring, her power waning. What would happen if she reached the limit of her endurance while her body remained immaterial?

Join with me . . . Though it had no words, she clearly understood the water's call. *Join with me forever* . . .

She tried to think. It didn't seem to matter how little water was present when she dematerialized, but when she had rematerialized before, she had been out in a lake, fully underwater when she reasserted her own shape . . .

Frantically she began casting around for the nearest body of water large enough to submerge her.

There! Not too far from Aunt Phyllis's house, a pool of some sort.

She emerged in hot, steaming water. She looked around.

Tile floor and walls. Stacks of towels. A frosted glass shower stall—

—and the blurred pink shape of someone—a *naked* someone!—on the other side of the glass! Ariane couldn't tell if it was a man or a woman, and didn't want to. *I'm in someone's hot tub!* she thought in horror.

She'd never moved so fast in her life. Up and out of the tub, ordering the water off of her body as she moved. Dry, she opened the door a crack and looked out into an empty hallway that ran deeper into the house to her right and ended at a door to her left—a door with shoes scattered around it, a sure sign it led outside.

Seconds later she stood gasping for breath in an alley, having set some kind of record for the twenty-five-metre dash. At last she knew exactly where she was. Aunt Phyllis's house also backed onto this alley, just a couple of trash bins to the north.

Unfortunately, Aunt Phyllis's house had a motion-activated light in the backyard. Ariane had hoped to sneak back in without being noticed, but her aunt must have seen the light come on. She opened the back door just as Ariane climbed the steps. "Ariane?" Aunt Phyllis looked bewildered. "How did you get here? You were upstairs taking a shower. I can still hear the water running . . ."

"I . . ." *Think fast!* ". . . um, thought I heard a, uh, cat. Meowing. Like it was hurt. Before I even got undressed. I went out to look. You must not have noticed. I guess I forgot to turn off the water." She hugged herself and pretended to shiver. "I didn't even stop to put on my coat."

"But . . ." Aunt Phyllis blinked at her, then shook her head and laughed. "Well, that book must be more engrossing than I realized . . . I never noticed a thing." She moved aside. "Did you find the cat?"

"What? Oh, no, no sign of it . . . guess I imagined it. Good night!"

Aunt Phyllis opened her mouth to say something else, but Ariane hurried past her without giving her the chance. The sooner she ended this conversation, the better.

A minute later she was standing in her bathroom again. She turned off the water and looked at herself in the now steamed-up mirror.

She *still* didn't look like a powerful sorceress. But after what she had just done . . .

It frightened her a little, but also emboldened her. Maybe she wasn't helpless against Merlin after all.

She wouldn't know until she tried to beat him. But she *would* try. The power of the Lady, the music of the water, the song of the sword—they were *hers*, something solid to hold on to, something that couldn't be taken away from her in an instant . . . as her mother had been. She knew where to find the first shard of Excalibur. She knew how to get there.

But could she take Wally with her?

Only one way to find out. She went into her room, turned on the light, and sat down at her computer. She opened her email software, entered Wally's address, and typed, *My idea worked. Meet me at the Human Bean tomorrow morning at 9:30?*

She clicked SEND. She leaned back in her chair, feeling an immense weariness. By the time her computer beeped, she had changed into her pyjamas and was brushing her teeth.

Wally's message was to the point. *I'll be there!—Wally.* He'd added a P.S. *Bring some of your Aunt Phyllis's cookies.*

Ariane laughed. And as she climbed into bed, it occurred to her she'd laughed more in the two days since she'd met Wally than she usually did in two months.

The thought didn't make her laugh again, but it did make her smile, as she drifted off to sleep.

❧   7   ❧

THE PONYTAILED MAN

The Learjet bucked like an angry horse as it descended through the clouds above Yellowknife, jerking up and down and from side to side as though determined to throw out its sole, white-knuckled passenger.

Rex Major gripped the arms of his seat and gritted his teeth. He hated flying—or rather, he hated flying in these cursed contraptions held up by nothing more substantial than air flowing around their wings, without a whiff of good solid magic. When he did have to fly—and in this strange age, it was necessary in order to conduct his business—he usually took Excalibur Computer System's Boeing 737, whose massive size he found comforting. But on this trip, the "optics," as his public relations advisor called it, dictated that he use the Learjet, whose luxurious interior was a plus but whose small dimensions he found alarming. By his using the Lear, owned by him personally rather than Rex Major Industries, his PR staff hoped to enhance the plausibility of his claim that he was making this trip purely out of curiosity.

As it was, the stock price of Thunderhill Diamonds Inc. had risen because of speculation that he was about to invest in the company. If he'd flown to Yellowknife in the ECS Boeing, complete with entourage, that price might have skyrocketed—and made it that much more expensive for him if he *did* decide to invest.

At the peak of his powers, he had loved to fly, sometimes putting his mind into a bird and soaring through the clouds on two honest, feathered wings—not like the ugly, rigid metallic things now holding them so tentatively in the air—sometimes simply rising from the ground in human form, using his magic to counteract the constant, hungry sucking of the Earth . . . gravity, they called it now.

Once he had re-forged Excalibur, claimed it as his own, and forced open the doorway between Earth and Faerie, he would fly like that again. But right now his powers were so diminished he couldn't even ensure that the metal monstrosity in whose belly he rode didn't immolate itself and him in one final angry plunge. If that happened, he would *die*, and all his ambitions with him. Though all-but-immune to aging, he could still be killed. And if he were, the Queen and Council of Clades might continue their tyranny over Faerie for another millennium, without challenge.

A lurch made him gasp and squeeze the armrests so hard his fingers turned white, but it was immediately followed by a second, softer lurch, and then the roar of the jet's engines, and he realized that while he had been busy convincing himself he was about to die, they had landed.

He looked out the window for his first glimpse of Yellowknife and saw nothing but swirling snow, lit intermittently by the flashing lights of the plane, as they taxied to the tiny terminal. A few moments later he was out in that storm, flipping up the collar of his overcoat and muttering two-thousand-year-old Faerie curses (the old ones were the best ones).

After that unpleasant interval, the terminal seemed almost homey. Hanging from the ceiling were banners the colour of northern skies and ice, a reminder that they weren't in the soft southland any more—as if the storm raging outside wasn't reminder enough. A tall, heavyset man with no hair on his head but lots on his chin approached, his hand outstretched.

"Mr. Major?"

Major shook the proffered hand. "Victor Ursu, I presume?"

"That's me. Vice-president for investor relations. It's a pleasure to meet you, sir." Ursu's deep voice, as big as the rest of him, boomed through the terminal. Major saw people turning to look, then whisper to each other, and knew he had been recognized. He sighed. As Merlin, he had often gone about his business incognito, but a millennium and a half ago he hadn't had to deal with mass media and the Internet splashing his photo all over the place.

Of course, he consoled himself, he was still incognito in the most important sense: nobody knew who he *really* was.

"What time tomorrow will we leave for the mine?" he asked.

Ursu shook his head. "I'm sorry, sir, but I don't think we'll be able to go tomorrow at all. This storm is going to get worse before it gets better. They're closing the airport. You made it in just under the wire."

Major was glad he hadn't had that knowledge a few minutes earlier, when he'd been gripping the arms of the

Learjet's seat. He felt a flash of annoyance at hearing it now. In the old days, no storm could have delayed him. "Then when *is* it expected to clear? I'm a busy man." It was a foolish thing to say. He knew Ursu could no more control the weather than he could . . . now. But his new persona as a hard-nosed businessman was so ingrained that phrases like that came to him almost automatically. They usually got results.

Not this time, of course. "I know you are, sir. And I'm sorry things turned out this way. But they're saying this storm won't let up until tomorrow night. It's a big one. Best we can hope for is to get out to the mine Monday morning."

Major sighed. "I assume my hotel has high-speed Internet access?"

Ursu nodded. "We made sure of that, sir."

"Then at least I can get some work done. Where are my bags?"

An extra day, he thought as Ursu led him to the baggage claim area. A stuffed polar bear snarled at him from a plaster ice floe at the centre of the carousel. Major bared his own teeth at the long-dead predator. *I've waited fifteen centuries. What's one more day?*

His hotel was nice enough, in a generic sort of way, though it fell far short of the plush accommodations to which he was accustomed. His usual hotel suites put the royal apartments in Camelot to shame—although in one sense, even the lowliest motel could say the same, since unlike Arthur and Guinevere's draughty rooms, modern motels had both running water *and* central heating.

And he had to admit, as he returned to his room late that night after a leisurely supper with Ursu in what he was told was the city's best restaurant, followed by a few drinks in the hotel lounge, that both food *and* wine were better in this age than they had been in Arthur's.

Feeling pleasantly stuffed and just a little tipsy, Major set up his laptop and checked his email. There were, as was usually the case after he'd been offline for a few hours, dozens. Several were flagged as urgent, but his eye immediately went to one from Keith Pritchard.

Pritchard had told him, the last time they had spoken by phone, that the magical program Major had sent him for his smartphone had worked like a charm, homing in on a young girl named Ariane Forsythe, little more than a child, the power of the Lady that clung to her drawing the magic in the smartphone app like a magnet. If she were the same person the Lady had tried to contact two and a half years ago, Major suspected the Lady's previous failure had been due to her young age. And the fact she was still so young, he'd thought, would make her easy to intimidate. He'd sent Pritchard another magical program, one that would deliver a terrifying warning right to the girl's computer. Major had fully expected that to be the end of the matter.

He opened the email, and discovered he was wrong.

I delivered the warning. I don't think it worked. The girl and that boy I told you about, the one she's been hanging out with, spent the evening on her computer. The tracer you had me put on her computer usage shows they were researching you.

Then, after the boy left, something very strange happened. There was a surge of magic, and then the girl vanished from the scanner completely. A few minutes later she showed up again, from outside the house, even though I never saw her leave.

I await your instructions.

Pritchard

Major stared at the email, feeling a sudden unfamiliar sensation: worry.

They spent the evening researching me? Then they've figured out I'm Merlin. And they must know I'm heading to the Thunderhill diamond mine. And that means . . .

"She knows," he whispered. "By the Tree, she knows where the shard is!"

And a surge of magic, followed by her disappearance, and then her return from an unexpected direction? It could only mean translocation.

Major swore. She didn't just have a *little* of the Lady's power. She had all of it—or at least much of it. He nervously fingered the ruby stud in his ear. *Magically, she's probably stronger than I am. She is the Lady of the Lake in this time and place, while I . . .*

While he, until he had Excalibur, could barely claim to still be Merlin.

But non-magically . . . non-magically, she was only a girl. And if she would not heed his warning . . . well, there were other ways to dissuade her.

The most direct method would be to have her killed, but that was impossible. The power of the Lady and the power of Excalibur were inextricably bound. Now that she had the Lady's power, if she were to die, at his hand or even accidentally, the power would die with her. Excalibur would become nothing but a rusting sword, the door to Faerie would slam shut, and he . . .

He would still be Rex Major, powerful, wealthy . . . but no longer ageless. Trapped outside of Faerie, with the door to its magic no longer even ajar, he would live out a normal human lifespan—then he, too, would die.

Killing her would be killing himself and all his hopes.

He was going to pull that ruby right out of his ear if he didn't quit fingering it. He forced himself to place his hands palms-down on the desk and hold them still.

Since he couldn't kill the girl, he could see only two possible ways to remove the threat she posed. One was to sequester her until it was too late for her to act against him. In a way, he liked that better than killing her: it echoed his own centuries-long imprisonment, imposed on him with the help of the Lady of the Lake. The Lady might be beyond the reach of an appropriate revenge, but her heir was not.

The second way was through fear. He didn't know what the Lady had told her. Quite possibly she didn't *know* that he couldn't kill her; if that were the case he could at least make her fear for her life. After all, just because he couldn't kill her, that didn't mean he couldn't hurt her . . . badly. And he could also make her fear for the lives of those close to her —the boy, for instance. Her loved ones were not protected by the power.

Abduction first, I think, he decided. *Lock her away and she will no longer be a threat.*

He had already Commanded Pritchard to obey all his instructions, no matter what the sacrifice to himself, so his minion would certainly do what must be done. Major sighed. *A pity to lose him, but I can easily replace him.* And lose

Pritchard he most likely would. If—when—he was caught, he would serve a very long sentence in prison for kidnapping a teenage girl.

Ah, well. An operative in prison might be useful.

And if Pritchard failed . . . well, there was still fear. She had a computer, and that computer could serve as a doorway, for him, or for . . . something else.

He smiled. Then he picked up his cell phone and dialled Pritchard's number.

Ariane started awake and sat up in bed.

Grey morning light filtered through the curtains. She could hear Aunt Phyllis singing "Oh What a Beautiful Morning" downstairs, accompanied by Pendragon meowing for his breakfast, but none of those things had awakened her.

What had jerked her out of sleep was a dream. As she had done the night before, she had been rushing through pipes and drains and streams and lakes, water among water, but unlike the night before, she had been unable to find any way home, anywhere where she could re-form her body, and she had felt herself growing thinner and thinner, more diluted, until she had been on the verge of vanishing completely . . .

She shuddered, and threw off the covers, glad for once to be getting out of bed early on a Sunday.

She pulled on her favourite old jeans and a worn-but-warm Saskatchewan Roughriders sweatshirt. She checked her email. Nothing from Wally.

After a stop in the bathroom—no surprises when she

touched the water—she descended to the kitchen. Aunt Phyllis, wearing a pink terrycloth bathrobe over a long flannel nightgown, turned from the counter and held out her favourite rose-patterned teapot. "Good morning, dear. You're up earlier than usual. Would you like some tea?"

"No, thanks. I'm supposed to meet Wally at the Human Bean for a latte." Trying to ignore Aunt Phyllis's raised eyebrows, she hurried on, "We're going to talk about our project." She remembered Wally's request. "Oh, yeah—and can I take some of those cookies you made last night?"

"Of course, dear. But dress warm! It frosted last night and the radio said it's barely going to get above freezing today. We might even get snow."

Ariane knew exactly how cold the night had been, having been splashing around in a prairie lake in the middle of it. But she couldn't very well tell Aunt Phyllis that. "I will." She gave Pendragon's head a good scratch, then headed out.

The Human Bean was a coffee shop located in an old house seven or eight blocks from Ariane's home. It was within easy walking distance of Oscana Collegiate and St. Dunstan's High, which made it a favourite of the smallish coffee-drinking subset of the high school crowd . . . but not on a Sunday morning, when most of her fellow students were sound asleep. Ariane didn't really care if anyone saw her with Wally, but she thought it might be better for Wally if no one saw him with her.

Oh, who am I kidding? she thought as she headed down the front walk, carrying a dozen of Aunt Phyllis's cookies in a brown paper bag. A thin layer of frost had made the concrete slippery, and gave it and the still slightly green grass bordering it a pale, washed-out look. Her breath rose in white clouds. The tipsy gnome under the spruce looked as cold and miserable as she had been when she'd crawled out of the lake. *Wally and I couldn't be worse social outcasts if we came down with Ebola.*

As she crossed College Avenue she heard a car start up behind her. Ariane stiffened, and a chill that had nothing to do with the frosty morning ran up her spine. From the far side of the street, she glanced back, half-expecting to see a white Ford Focus headed her way. But she relaxed when she saw it was just a blue Saturn, turning onto College.

Nothing to do with me, she told herself as she walked west. Sure enough, the Saturn drove past without slowing down, turned north, and disappeared.

Relieved, she crossed Winnipeg Street at the light, then turned north for one block before heading west again. As she turned the corner, her foot skidded on the frost-covered side-walk and she almost fell. She gasped, caught herself, and then laughed ruefully. It'd be the height of irony if she broke her leg walking to the coffee shop before she'd even started her dangerous quest.

A little more carefully, she carried on. Once she was past the hospital, she turned north again. The Human Bean was just a couple of blocks ahead.

To her right, red and orange leaves, interspersed with shrivelled, purplish-black berries, still clung to a high hedge. Behind it rose a dilapidated two-storey house. Just before she reached the hedge, the blue Saturn shot out backwards from a driveway behind the hedge and jerked to a tire-chirping stop, blocking the sidewalk. The driver's door burst open, and a tall man, grey-bearded and ponytailed, dressed in jeans and a denim jacket, burst from the driver's seat and dashed around the back of the car.

Ariane froze, but the frost saved her. The man's foot slipped out from under him and he fell against the car, grabbing the side-view mirror for support. Ariane regained control of her muscles and ran into the street. The man swore and charged after her. She could hear his feet hitting the pavement just three or four metres behind her. *His legs are longer. He's faster than me—*

—but maybe not as agile!

She cut left into an empty driveway. A leap over a hedge landed her in a weed-grown backyard, and she scrambled over a low fence of weathered wood into the alley beyond. Her pursuer dropped back. A clatter and a curse suggested he had fallen over the fence, but before she reached the end of the alley, she could hear the crunching sound of his feet grinding against gravel. Once again he was drawing closer and closer.

She burst onto a street. Tires squealed as a car braked hard to avoid her. She dodged around its tail and ran into the alley across the street. She was hoping her pursuer wouldn't follow her with a potential witness in the car, but he didn't stop. Still, the car had blocked him long enough that she gained a little ground. Halfway down the alley she spotted a narrow path leading between two houses on her right. She darted through it, dashed across another street, and plunged between two more houses into the next alley.

When she glanced back, she couldn't see the man anymore. She slackened her pace, trying to catch her breath. Twenty more steps . . . thirty . . . no sign of him. She slowed even more, looking back down the alley as she came abreast of a dilapidated garage with leaning walls and peeling green paint. She became aware of something in her hand, glanced down, and laughed shakily when she saw that she was still clutching the brown paper bag containing Aunt Phyllis's cookies.

But then she screamed and dropped the bag as the man burst out from behind the garage. He grabbed her arm and pulled her to him, then clamped his free hand tightly over her mouth, choking off her scream. He forced her arm up behind her back. "I'm not going to hurt you," he growled in her ear, though he already was. "But you have to come with me."

She tried to struggle, but he jerked her arm up higher, making her gasp. He began dragging her down the alley, back toward his car. She rolled her eyes, searching for water . . . if she could find water, she could do something . . . but there wasn't so much as a puddle.

"Hey!" someone shouted. "Let her go!" The man twisted them both around, and her heart leaped when she saw Wally charging toward them, carrying something that looked like a sword.

WALLY HAD ARRIVED twenty minutes earlier than he needed to at the Human Bean. He had long suffered from the curse of punctuality, so he was used to waiting for other people to show up. And getting out of the house early was always the best way to avoid crossing paths with Flish, especially on weekends.

When he reached the Human Bean, Wally decided to

wait for Ariane on the sidewalk. He only had enough money for one cup of coffee, and he didn't want to finish it before Ariane got there. The rotund proprietor of the coffee shop was okay with kids lounging if they had bought stuff, but he didn't much care for them "just hanging out."

Wally didn't mind the chill in the air—he'd always kind of liked the cold. He amused himself with a broken hockey stick he found lying in the gutter, practising fencing moves with it, although of course it was much heavier than an epée or even a sabre, and the balance was all wrong . . . not that he was a good enough swordsman for that to matter. His recently sprained wrist didn't even twinge. That was good, he supposed, except it meant he'd have to go back to gym class.

After a few minutes, he wandered to the corner, still clutching the hockey stick, to see if Ariane was in sight. He looked down the street and up the avenue, but didn't see her. He was about to return to his post on the sidewalk when he spotted a familiar figure in the alley—*Ariane?* Just as he was going to call out to her, a man with a grey ponytail leaped out from behind a garage and grabbed her arm. Ariane's scream broke off abruptly. "Hey!" Hefting the hockey stick, Wally charged across the street. "Let her go!"

The man twisted around to face him, holding Ariane's arm pinned behind her with one hand and keeping his other hand over her mouth. "Mind your own business, kid!"

"She's my friend!" Wally skidded to a stop and gripped the hockey stick tighter, pointing it at the man. "Let her go!"

"I'm warning you . . ." the man growled—and then yelped when Wally whacked his left elbow with the stick. He released Ariane in surprise, and grunted when the stick jabbed his stomach—Wally had meant to hit him harder, but his target had pulled back.

Ariane darted to one side, out of the man's reach. Wally advanced *en garde*. "Next one is below the belt!"

The man spat out an expletive and tried to grab the stick, but Wally danced aside, and as the man's hands closed on empty air, he stumbled, falling to his hands and knees. Wally kicked one arm out from under him and gave him a backhanded whack to the rear. The man fell down face-first.

"Didn't say where below the belt, did I?" Wally said.

Ariane's attacker staggered to his feet and raised a hand to his bloody nose. Wally held the stick ready in case he attacked again. The man gave Wally one last glare, and then ran away without a word, ponytail bouncing.

Wally hurried back to Ariane.

"Are you all right?"

"I'm fine," she said. Considering her pale face, Wally was pretty sure she was lying. "He didn't hurt me. In fact he promised he wouldn't."

"We should call the police . . ."

"No!"

Wally stared at her. "No? A strange man just grabbed you and you don't want to tell the police? What if he grabs someone else?"

Ariane shook her head. "It's only me he's after."

"You sound like you know him." Wally felt a sudden surge of suspicion. "He's not a, a drug dealer or something like that?"

Ariane's laughter carried only a slight tinge of hysteria. "You watch too much TV."

"Only news, documentaries and science fiction," Wally said, relieved. "So who is he, then?"

"I don't know his name, but I know who he works for." Ariane took a deep breath. "Rex Major."

Wally stared in the direction the man had run off. "He was the guy who was parked outside your house when the computer went crazy?"

"Unless there are two old guys with ponytails stalking me, yeah."

"But you should still call the police! Even if he's not a threat to anyone else, he's a threat to *you*."

"If we have him arrested, Rex Major will know we know he's after us. I'd rather keep him in the dark."

"Don't you think he already knows we know he's after us?"

"He may know we know *Merlin* is after us. But he may not know we know he, Major, is Merlin."

Wally groaned. "My head hurts."

"Look," Ariane said, "right now Merlin has all the advantages. So anything I know that he doesn't, or at least that he doesn't know I know . . . maybe it will help. Right now he may not even know that I know he's Rex Major. I'd like to keep it that way."

Now that the adrenalin was draining away, Wally felt a little shaky. If he could see himself, he might even be as pale as Ariane. *What if that guy had had a knife? Or a gun?* His heroics with the broken hockey stick could have gotten them both killed.

For the first time, Wally realized that a quest in the real world might involve real danger. *Uncomfortable things, adventures. Might make you late for dinner . . .*

. . . or worse.

But he was only the . . . the sidekick. Ariane was the freaking Lady of the Lake. The decision was hers. *Wally's First Law of Sidekickery: The heroine is always right.* He grinned, but the grin dissolved in dismay when something close to his feet caught his eye: a brown paper bag, ripped and stepped-on, from which spilled . . .

"Oh no! Don't tell me!"

Ariane followed his gaze, and sighed. "I'm afraid so. Aunt Phyllis's cookies."

"That was going to be my breakfast!"

"Cheer up!" Ariane gave him a friendly shove back up the alley. "There are cinnamon buns at the Human Bean . . . and I'm buying." She grinned. Colour had returned to her face—she looked more like her usual self. "Because I know something else Rex Major doesn't know I know."

"What?" Wally gave the crushed cookies one last, woeful glance over his shoulder.

"I know how to use the Lady's power to get to the shard of Excalibur. I tested it last night. Major doesn't know it yet, but he's in a race—and *we're* going to win it."

"Really?" Wally matched her grin. "Tell me about it . . . over cinnamon buns."

He led the way back toward the Human Bean. But he didn't let go of the broken hockey stick.

A DIP IN HUDSON BAY

THE YELLOW WALLS and antique-filled interior of the Human Bean felt invitingly cozy to Ariane after her chilling adventure in the alley. She ordered a large skim-milk latte for herself and a large iced cappuccino for Wally (*Brrr!* she thought), plus two cinnamon buns (heated), and settled down in one of the coffee shop's overstuffed couches. Wally sat down on another, on the other side of a low table painted with goofy black and white cows against a green background. It could have been any ordinary Sunday morning.

But Ariane's hand trembled as she raised her latte to her lips. What would have happened if Wally hadn't shown up? How far was Rex Major willing to go to stop her?

As if you don't know. Major might be impersonating a modern businessman, but he wasn't one. They had to remember that. He was a millennia-old sorcerer—Merlin, no less—from a time when human life was even cheaper than it was in the twenty-first century. He'd kill her (or have her killed) the instant he seriously thought she might interfere with his search for the shards of Excalibur.

But as that frightening thought crossed her mind, she frowned. Except . . .

Why hadn't he done it already? Why had he even bothered with that bizarre computer-borne warning? The ponytailed man who had attacked her had been hanging around her house for two days. He'd followed her to the convenience store. He'd had several opportunities to run her over, if he'd wanted to kill her. But he hadn't. And even today, he'd said, "I'm not going to hurt you . . ."

She found that slightly comforting . . . but only slightly. Even assuming she could believe him, and he hadn't just been trying to stop her from struggling, he'd at least been out to kidnap her. While as a potential victim she wholeheartedly endorsed kidnapping over murder, she'd much rather not experience either one.

And then she gripped her mug tightly in horror. That ponytailed creep *knew where she lived*. That meant he knew about Aunt Phyllis. What if he hurt Aunt Phyllis trying to get to her, or just to teach her a lesson, like they did in movies? The liquid in Ariane's mug sloshed as her hand quivered. She put down her latte and pushed her cinnamon bun away—she no longer had an appetite.

Wally eyed her plate. "I'll eat that if you don't want it." He'd apparently inhaled his own bun. Whatever nerves he'd felt after the encounter with the ponytailed man—and he'd been white as a freckle-faced ghost for a few minutes—had obviously gone away.

"Be my guest."

Wally picked up the bun, but didn't bite into it right

away. "What's wrong? You look like you just tasted something rotten."

Ariane told him what she'd been thinking. "I'm not worried about myself. Well, OK, I am, a bit. But if anything happened to Aunt Phyllis because of me . . ."

"*Now* are you ready to call the police?" Wally took a big bite of the cinnamon bun. "I told you . . . mmmm . . . we should have called them right away . . . mmph."

"It's going to be our word against . . . whoever that guy is," Ariane said. "Why should the police believe *me*? I'm what they call 'troubled,' you know. Father ran out years ago, mother vanished mysteriously, bounced from foster home to foster home and school to school before my aunt took me in. I'm not what the cops are going to call a reliable witness, and that guy, if he works for Rex Major, has a respectable tax-paying position with Excalibur Computer Systems. They'll think I'm making it all up to gain attention."

"But I'll tell them—"

"They'll think *you're* making it up to gain attention too."

Wall blinked. "I don't—"

She sighed, and in the tone of a daycare teacher explaining to a toddler for the umpteenth time why it's important to wash one's hands after using the potty, she said, "*My* attention, Wally. They'll think you're in love with me, or something."

Wally turned the approximate colour of a ripe tomato. "That's nuts!"

Ariane felt a little annoyed. "Of course it is." Now it was Wally's turn to frown. "But they won't know that."

"But if you really think your Aunt Phyllis is in danger, what else can you do?"

Ariane hadn't known, until that moment, but Wally's straightforward question crystallized the answer in her mind. "I have to leave," she said slowly. "I have to run away."

IT TOOK a lot to distract Wally from a fresh cinnamon bun, but Ariane's declaration succeeded. He stared at her, bun in hand and mouth wide open, for a long moment, then put the bun down unbitten. "That's crazy!"

Ariane looked pale, but she lifted her chin stubbornly. "Why? If I'm gone, if I leave Regina, then Rex Major won't have any reason to hurt Aunt Phyllis."

"Of course he will!" Wally said. "If he's going to hurt her to make you abandon the quest, he's just as likely to do it if you leave town as he is if you stay put." Ariane opened her mouth as though she were going to argue, and he hurried on, fiercely telling the inner voice reminding him about *Wally's First Law of Sidekickery* that sometimes the heroine *wasn't* right, and this was one of those times. "You can't protect her by leaving. In fact, with your power, you're more likely to be able to protect her by staying put. And anyway, whether she'd be safer or not if you left, *you're* safer here with people who can help—like me."

Ariane met his gaze squarely. "Hasn't it occurred to you I'm putting *you* in danger too?"

"Occurred to me?" He snorted. "I just fought some guy in an alley. Of course it's occurred to me! But I don't care."

And he didn't. Whatever risk he ran by helping Ariane seemed minor compared to the risk of never seeing her again if she ran away. Wally had always thought he was happy as a loner, but he didn't want to be one anymore. Ariane was his friend, and he didn't intend to lose her. "And anyway, the same thing applies to me. Rex Major won't leave me *or* Aunt Phyllis alone just because you run away. We'll still be in danger, and you'll just be in *more* danger."

Ariane closed her eyes. "You're right. I know you're right. It's just . . . I didn't mean to get Aunt Phyllis involved. But there's no getting out of it, is there? She . . . and you . . . and I . . . are all at risk until we have Excalibur and Merlin doesn't."

"Or until he has it!"

Ariane stared at him.

"I mean it, Ariane! Why not just *let him have it?* Take his warning. Forget about the whole thing." Wally surprised himself with his vehemence. *What about the quest?* a part of him protested, but he ignored it. *Screw the quest.* "Don't look at me that way. This is getting serious! At first it was kind of fun, like a movie or a video game or playing make-believe—a little adventure you can quit when Mom calls you for dinner. But someone tried to kidnap you—or worse. And now you're talking about running away from home. Let Merlin have the stupid sword. We didn't ask for any of this! It's none of our business."

Ariane was silent for a moment. "I can't," she finally said. She looked down into her coffee cup. "I just can't."

"Why?" Wally said. "So Merlin wants to be king of the world. So what? Maybe we should let him! Maybe that's what we need on this stupid planet. Maybe he could put an end to the wars in the Middle East and Africa and wherever else we're killing each other this week. Heck, he's a sorcerer. Maybe he could put an end to famine and poverty and disease while he's at it." He recalled what else had occurred to him. "Jeez, Ariane . . . did you ever think that maybe we're on the wrong side? Maybe *Merlin* is the good guy. Maybe the Lady of the Lake is the villain in this story we've been sucked into, and we're just . . . pawns."

Ariane shook her head furiously. "No! Merlin would be a dictator, Wally. We might have peace and food and health —*might*, because we don't know if Merlin has that much power—but we'd also have secret police and show trials and political prisoners . . . and there'd be no Amnesty International to complain to, either, because no one would be allowed to criticize the High King. Wally, you're the history buff. What did the old-time kings do to anyone who posed the slightest threat to their kingship?"

"They executed them," Wally said impatiently. "But Merlin is a sorcerer! No one could seriously threaten his kingship except . . ." He suddenly saw what she was getting at. "Oh," he finished in a small voice.

Ariane nodded. "*Oh.* Except someone else with magical powers. And the only person we know of besides Merlin who has magical powers is . . . *me.*"

The cinnamon bun he'd already eaten congealed into a solid lump of indigestible dough in Wally's stomach. "He'll kill you."

"Probably."

"Then . . ." Wally swallowed. "That man who grabbed you—he didn't want to just kidnap you, he wanted to . . ." his voice trailed off.

Ariane frowned. "I don't know, Wally. He said he wouldn't hurt me. He might have been lying, of course, but . . . I think—I hope—that maybe there's some reason Major doesn't want to kill me yet. Maybe he needs something from me." She shook her head. "But even putting aside what Major—Merlin—might do with Excalibur . . . I can't give up the quest, Wally. Not now that I have the Lady's power. Excalibur is . . ." She broke off. "It's hard to explain," she said after a minute. "But I can't let him have it. I *can't.*"

Wally pushed away the remains of Ariane's cinnamon bun. It no longer looked appetizing. "Major has been up at the Thunderhill Diamond Mine since yesterday. He may already have the first shard."

"He doesn't. I'd know it if he did." Ariane paused, looking a little puzzled. "I don't know *how* I'd know. But I know I would. I need to get up there. I need to get up there *today.*"

"And you think you know how? That's what 'it worked' meant in your email?"

"Yeah. But I warn you, it's pretty weird . . ."

Wally snorted. "Weirder than everything else that has happened?"

Ariane smiled a little. "I guess not."

But as he listened to what she had done, Wally thought she'd guessed wrong. "Let me get this straight," he said. "You stuck your hands into the water, and you . . . dissolved? Went down the drain?"

"Yeah," Ariane said. "I guess so."

"But to . . . um, pull yourself together, you had to be somewhere with enough water to cover you."

"Yeah . . ."

"Why?" Wally said. He laughed at her startled look. "Well, *why?* If you're already violating the law of conservation of mass and energy, why can't you do whatever you want? This is magic, right? No rules!"

"There are rules," Ariane said. "They're just not the ones we're used to."

"But what are they?" Wally scratched his head. "I mean, there has to be a cost. TANSTAAFL."

"TAN-what? Speak English."

"TANSTAAFL. There Ain't No Such Thing As A Free Lunch." Ariane frowned, and he hurried on. "Never mind. So this water-teleporting, or whatever, works for you. The question is, can you take me with you?"

Ariane looked out the window into the cold grey street. "I think I can. I don't think I should."

"What?" Wally stared at her. "Why?"

She turned her gaze back to him. "Because this is dangerous, Wally. Even if Major needs me alive for some reason, he doesn't need you."

"But you do!" Wally shot back. *She's offering you an out,* a cowardly part of him noted. *You could agree with her, forget this whole thing, stay safe . . .*

Forget? Forget meeting the Lady of the Lake? Forget that Rex Major is Merlin, that Excalibur is out there, that Ariane is trying to find it? Are you nuts?

"You need me," he continued, his voice low and intense. "To talk to. To carry things. To Google stuff. To whack the bad guys with hockey sticks. To . . . I don't know what else. And neither do you. You can't do this alone, Ariane!"

Her lower lip trembled and for a horrible moment he thought he had made her cry. But when she spoke, her voice was steady. "I know. I just . . . I don't want you to get hurt."

"Well, there's something we agree on, anyway," he said,

and was rewarded with a small smile. "So. No more argument. I'm coming with you . . ." He paused. "Um . . . if you really can take me along, that is."

"It seems like I should be able to." Ariane's uncertain tone didn't exactly fill him with confidence. "But until we try it, I won't know for sure."

"Your clothes went with you?"

"What—oh! I see what you mean. If my clothes went with me, then maybe I can take anything I'm touching." She nodded. "Yes, they went with me."

An intriguing vista of interesting possibilities vanished from Wally's imagination. "Oh, well . . ." Ariane raised an eyebrow at him, and he hurried on. "Logically, it should work, then. Except, of course, we're talking magic, so logic may not have anything to do with it." Oddly, the cinnamon bun looked appetizing again. He pulled it back toward his side of the table, picked it up, and took a huge bite out of it. "S'whedyawanuryt?"

Ariane gave him a puzzled (and slightly disgusted) look. He hastily chewed and swallowed. "Sorry. Where do you want to try it?"

"I'm not sure. It has to be somewhere private, and Aunt Phyllis is home—we can't do it there. And we need a large body of water to materialize in when we return. Large enough to submerge both of us. I don't think a bathtub will do it—not for two of us."

Wally nodded. "My house, then. You probably didn't notice the indoor pool—"

"You have an indoor pool?" Ariane's voice implied she had never expected to be friends with someone who had his own swimming pool. Wally felt embarrassed.

"Yeah, just a little one, but big enough for both of us to, um, materialize in." *I feel like I've fallen into* Star Trek, Wally thought. "Better yet, Ms. Carson is at church, and Felicia won't crawl out of bed for hours yet." Wally stuffed the rest of the cinnamon bun in his mouth. "Tinfinitynbond!"

Back to being a faithful sidekick, he thought a few minutes later as they left the Human Bean. He couldn't argue with Ariane's logic. If Merlin succeeded in setting himself up as King of the World, Ariane would be a threat to his power. He might need her alive now for some magical reason, but after he'd won . . . he would kill her. Or at least imprison her. No question. Abandoning the quest would only buy her a brief reprieve, not a full pardon.

But in the back of his mind, a little seed of doubt still lingered.

How do we know we can trust the Lady of the Lake any more than we can trust Rex Major?

Another phrase from Tolkien came to mind: *Do not meddle in the affairs of wizards . . .*

He snorted. *Good advice. But it looks like we don't have a choice.*

HALF AN HOUR after leaving the Human Bean, Ariane and Wally stood on the edge of the Knights' swimming pool, about to try something that, even though she knew she had done it the night before, seemed completely nuts in the cold light of morning.

But, like the Queen in *Alice in Wonderland,* she was

getting used to believing several impossible things before breakfast . . . or just slightly after breakfast, in this case.

As promised, Ms. Carson was at church and Felicia still asleep. They'd crept through the house silent as mice to ensure she stayed that way. Now Wally looked around the cedar-walled room, dimly lit by the blue-green glow of the submerged lights around the edges of the pool. "So what do we do?"

"Jump in," Ariane said.

"With our clothes on?"

Ariane gave him an over-sweet smile. "Well, I'm keeping mine on. I guess you can take yours off if you want to . . ."

He blushed. "Uh, no."

"All right then." She looked at the water. "On three. One . . . two . . . three!"

They splashed into the water simultaneously. It came up to Ariane's chest, and almost to Wally's shoulders. "I just feel silly," Wally said. He pushed wet hair out of his face. "Now what?"

"Just . . . be quiet." Ariane closed her eyes, listening to the song of the water, urging her to join in, to flow and frolic with it to river, lake, and sea. And mixed in with it . . . yes, there it was. Distant, faint, but unmistakable and exciting: the song of the sword. Keeping her eyes closed, she reached out to Wally. "Hold on," she said.

Wally said something as he took her hand, but it was lost in the sudden whirling surge of water as she gave herself over to its call and let it carry her away . . .

. . . no, not just her, both of them. She could feel another presence with her in the rush and tumble of the water, holding on to her for dear life, and for a moment she resented it. She didn't *want* to share the water with anyone else. She wanted to brush off the offending presence, let it swirl away into nothingness, but faint alarm bells rang in her mind at the thought. *That's Wally . . . it worked . . . he's* supposed to *be here . . .* What would happen if she did break loose from him? Would he materialize somewhere or would he simply dissolve, never to be seen again?

That horrifying thought snapped her back to her senses. They had been rushing along with the water with no aim or control. Now she cast around for some clue as to their whereabouts, and with some strange sense she had no name for—not quite sight, not quite smell, not quite hearing, and yet with elements of all three—she knew they were in the same lake she'd materialized in the night before, and realized it must be Buffalo Pound Lake, the reservoir that provided Regina's drinking water.

Farther, she thought. *Let's see how far we can go . . .*

Onward. She found the Qu'Appelle River outlet on the other side of the dam, and took it, following the water from river to river to river, over rocks, over waterfalls, through the great inland freshwater sea that was Lake Winnipeg, out into the Nelson River. The song of the sword began to grow too, as they moved north, but she still couldn't quite pinpoint its source. She exerted more power. They streaked through the water like twin meteors crossing the night sky. Swirling currents, waterfalls, rapids, all meant nothing to the power of the Lady of the Lake . . . they sped through them as if they weren't there. North . . . north . . . north, the sword calling to her . . . and then she sensed that it was no longer just north, but off to the northwest . . .

. . . and then they hit Hudson Bay.

Once when Ariane was ten years old and dashing down a sidewalk she had turned her head at the wrong moment and run into a telephone pole. More than the pain, she remembered the shock—the instant change from moving full flight to sitting motionless and bleeding on the sidewalk.

This was like that, but ten times worse. As soon as the water changed from fresh to salt, her power deserted her. With an explosion of spray, their bodies materialized. By instinct, she kicked, and her head burst out into the open air.

Wrapped in the cocoon of her power, she had been oblivious to the temperature of the water through which they raced. Now cold gripped her with breath-stopping suddenness. To her left she glimpsed a grey sky. Tossing waves stretched to the indistinct horizon, lost in a haze of distant rain, or snow. To her right she saw a shore as barren as the surface of Mars.

A hand still gripped hers, pulling her down . . .

"Let go!" she spluttered, jerking at it. The hand released her. Her head sank beneath the water at the same instant, but her feet were touching the bottom, and when she straightened up, her head and shoulders broke out into the frigid air. She heard coughing and saw Wally glaring at her.

"Not exactly first-class travel!" A wave splashed into his mouth, and he choked and sputtered. "Take us h-home!"

She reached for the power . . . and couldn't find it.

Saltwater. She could feel it on her skin, but to her power it was invisible. *Lady of the Lake, not Lady of the Ocean . . .*

"I can't," Ariane shouted. "I can't do anything with salt water. We have to find the river that brought us here. It c-can't be far away. Let's get onto the sh-shore." Ariane's teeth were chattering.

They splashed onto the rock-strewn shore. Again Ariane reached for her power, intending to order the water off both their bodies . . . and again she failed. She felt a pang of fear. "I may h-have made a s-serious mi-mistake. We could f-f-freeze out here."

"Not if I h-have anyth-thing to s-say about it." Wally looked around. Ariane followed his gaze. Rocks. Water. Clouds. A high bluff that blocked the view inland. "How far n-north are we?"

"S-southern end of H-Hudson Bay, I th-think."

"Still s-south of the tree line, then. Let's c-climb up there," he pointed to the top of the bluff, "and see what's what. It'll help k-keep us warm, if n nothing else."

They scrambled up the steep slope. The exercise did make Ariane feel a little—a *very* little—warmer. As their heads cleared the top of the bluff, Wally whooped. "Trees! Come on." He scrambled over the lip of the bluff and onto the level ground beyond, then pulled her up after him.

"You've got m-matches?" Ariane said, her teeth starting to chatter again.

"No, but I've got something better." Wally grinned at her. "A knife—and knowledge."

Puzzled, but hoping desperately Wally knew what he was doing, Ariane followed him through the trees. At least here they were out of the wind's reach. Wally cast around on the ground for dry wood, and built a pyramid of good-sized sticks over a small pile of twigs. In the centre he scraped dry, powdery punk from the underside of a dead log. Then he searched the ground until he found two branches, one quite thick, the other little more than a stick. He came back to

Ariane and sat cross-legged, placing the branches in front of him.

"Willow," he said, patting the thicker branch. "Softwood." With his pocketknife, he carved a groove in it. Then he picked up the stick. "Tamarack," he said. "Hardwood." He shaped the end of it, then braced the thicker branch on his hip, slipped the stick into the groove, and began rubbing it back and forth, pressing down. Within moments he was breathing hard and sweating.

"I can see how it m-makes *you* warmer," Ariane said, "b-but it's not doing m-much for *m-me*."

"Give it time," Wally panted. To Ariane's amazement, a tendril of smoke rose from where the sticks met, and the wood dust that had formed in the groove in the willow branch began to glow. Quickly, Wally scraped the glowing dust onto the dry, rotted wood he'd already put in the middle of his pyramid. A tiny flame licked up. The twigs ignited, then the larger sticks, and moments later, a fire was blazing cheerfully at Ariane's feet.

She plopped down on the ground beside it, so close her clothes steamed in the chill air. As the warmth seeped into her bones, she realized she was exhausted. Not just physically, but mentally and in some other way she could hardly put a name to. Magically? Spiritually? Whatever reservoirs of inner strength she relied on to guide the Lady's power were empty. She could feel her strength seeping back, but slowly . . . so slowly.

"Maybe if I had something to eat . . ." she said, thinking out loud. "I'm starving."

Wally frowned, then suddenly brightened. He dug into

the right pocket of his jeans and held out a small plastic box. "Tic Tac?"

Ordinarily Ariane hated mints, but she grabbed the box and poured the entire contents into her mouth, chewing and swallowing them in moments. "That's better. But . . ." She gave Wally an apologetic look. "I can't send us back. Not for a while. I've got to get my strength back."

"Told you," Wally said. "TANSTAAFL. 'There Ain't No Such Thing As A Free Lunch.'"

"Too bad, because I could sure use a free lunch right about now," Ariane said. She looked at him hopefully. "Anything else to eat in those pockets of yours?"

"Not unless you like lint. But I'll see what I can find in the forest." Wally got to his feet. "Wait here."

"Don't get lost."

"I won't. A-plus in orienteering." He moved off among the trees, and disappeared from sight.

Ariane couldn't keep her head up—the heat from the fire had relaxed all her muscles. The ground was covered with spruce needles, but she curled up on it anyway. It was hard and the needles were sharp, but she was so tired . . .

She jerked awake an indeterminate time later to find Wally crouching on his heels beside her, holding out a branch covered with berries. "Arctic Bilberry," he said. "Pretty much dried out, this time of year, but there ought to be some nutrition in them. Think of them as raisins. That's about the best I can do." He looked grave. "You'd better be able to get us back, or we're going to get very hungry very soon."

The berries, small and shrivelled, were the most delicious-looking things Ariane had ever seen. She stripped the branch of them, stuffing them into her mouth. They took a lot of chewing, but again she felt a surge of power within her. Between the berries and the sleep . . .

"I think we can try it," Ariane said. "Even if I can't get us all the way home, I can get us most of the way . . . somewhere with people, anyway."

"Then let's go." Wally jerked his head toward the western horizon, where the sky was several shades darker than the light grey clouds overhead. "I think there's a storm coming. I really don't want to be here when it hits."

Ariane nodded. "We have to find the river," she said. She went to the top of the bluff and looked both ways along the rock-strewn shore. It was hard to spot anything among the tumble of boulders, but something silvery-white caught her eye. She squinted, and caught a hint of movement, the flicker of water foaming across submerged stones. "There!" She pointed.

Together they clambered back down the bluff and picked their way through the stones until they reached the mouth of the river, where the water poured over wet rock into Hudson Bay. Ariane hesitated. The white-flecked, steel-grey water looked as cold and sharp as a frozen knife blade, and her flesh recoiled at the thought of stepping into it . . . but she remembered how the icy water of Wascana Lake had felt milk-warm around her bare feet. Maybe she didn't have to worry about how cold water—well, fresh water, anyway—was anymore. At least, not when she was fully charged.

She snorted. *What am I, a battery?*

Wally didn't have that protection, of course, and she felt sorry for him, but it wasn't like there was any choice. She held out her hand to Wally. He took it, his fingers as cold as the air around them, and she waded in.

Sure enough, the water felt warm and comforting to her, though she heard Wally gasp. She kept walking until the water reached her knees. "Here we go." She closed her eyes, reached for the power . . . and felt herself become one with the water.

Or two, counting Wally.

It was harder to make headway this time, heading upstream . . . up rivers, through dams. They passed through Buffalo Pound Lake, through the water treatment plant, followed the pipes into the city . . .

Her strength began to fail again. She hadn't had as much to start with, and now she was losing the sense of where she was. She couldn't find Wally's house, couldn't . . .

. . . no, wait, *there*—the pool they had started from. Out through the jets, and . . .

Ariane's feet hit the bottom of the pool. She stood up, sputtering and gasping as her head and shoulders emerged into the air, and she felt the familiar sting of chlorine in her eyes. Cedar walls surrounded them. Wally shoved his dripping hair out of his eyes and looked around. "Home, sweet home," he said. "You did it!"

With a sense of triumph, Ariane waded toward the pool's ladder. She climbed up onto the tile floor, just in front of the door leading to the rest of the house. Wally climbed out beside her. Finding she still had a little power left, Ariane ordered the water to depart. Liquid sprayed out from their bodies, soaking the walls, the floor, the towels on a rack by the door . . .

. . . and Felicia, who had opened the door at *precisely* the wrong moment and was staring at them open-mouthed and dripping. She wore a skimpy bikini (*If I had a figure like that, so would I*, Ariane thought with a pang of jealousy) and carried a large pink—and now very wet—towel.

Wally recovered first. "Hi, sis. Have a good sleep?"

Felicia's look of shock morphed into one of fury. "What is *she* doing here?"

Ariane was in no mood for Felicia's petty hatred. She raised her hand, and a tendril of water twisted snakelike out of the pool. Ariane flicked her hand forward, and the water tendril darted at Felicia, stopping just short of her nose. Felicia jerked back, banging her head on the doorpost.

"What's it to you?" Ariane snarled. "Last time I saw you, you were running for your life. Maybe you should start running again."

Wally's grin vanished. "Ariane. Please. She lives here, remember?"

"Yeah, I know, I've seen her lair." The water tendril snapped forward again, spraying Felicia's face. "Crawl back to it, Felicia. Crawl back to it, and don't bother me again."

Felicia's face was ash-white, and her voice strained. "Get her out of our house, Wally. Maybe I can't touch her—*yet*—but you *know* what I'll do to you."

Ariane resisted the urge to shove the tendril of pool water right down Felicia's throat. Besides, she could feel her energy draining away. In a moment, she wouldn't be able to control the tendril at all. So instead she flicked it once more at Felicia's face, then jerked her hand back. The water slipped back into the pool with a slurping sound.

Felicia glared at Ariane, fists clenched, then turned and

disappeared down the hall and through a door that revealed a brief glimpse of the laundry room before it slammed shut.

Ariane took a deep breath, then saw Wally glaring at her, too, his expression so much like Felicia's that for the first time she saw the family resemblance.

"What's wrong?" she asked.

WALLY'S HEART pounded in his chest. He dug his fingernails into the palms of his clenched hands. Anger, hot and unexpected, choked him as he tried to respond. All he managed to squeeze out of his tight throat was, "You'd better go."

Ariane looked puzzled. "All right. But if she does anything to you—"

"I can deal with her!"

Ariane blinked. "What's wrong?"

"Nothing. Nothing at all."

"Did I do something—"

"I don't need you to fight my battles for me!" The words exploded out of him. "I can handle Flish. I've been doing it for years."

"Really." Ariane's reply was cool. "I guess that's why she had you cleaning up her room."

"*Which I wouldn't have had to do if you hadn't trashed it!* Every time you two get in a catfight I'm the one she takes it out on. Why don't you just leave her alone?"

"After everything she's done "

"She's my sister!" *And until the last couple of years, she was my best friend.*

He expected Ariane to argue, but she surprised him. Her face softened. "Yes, she is," she said, her voice strangely wistful. "I never had a brother or a sister, Wally. I guess I don't understand how it is. I promise I'll leave her alone . . . but if she interferes . . ."

"That's all I ask." Wally willed himself to calm down. He unclenched his fists and even managed a small smile. "Thank you."

"Thank *you*. For the rescue this morning." She grinned at him, and Wally felt the last of his anger melt away. "You really are my 'Knight' in shining armour."

Wally groaned. "I wondered how long it would take before the puns on my last name started . . ."

"Hey, you're lucky I put it off this long." She laughed. "Anyway, you're right, I should go." She turned serious. "So . . . now you know what it's like . . . are you really coming with me tonight? To the diamond mine? Last chance to back out."

Wally's heart raced. He still wasn't entirely convinced they could trust the Lady. Travelling through the water with Ariane had been terrifying, and the thought of a face-to-face confrontation with Rex Major—Merlin!—was more frightening yet. But there was no way he was going to let Ariane go by herself. "I'm coming. But I don't want to get caught off-guard like we were this afternoon. We should take some camping equipment with us . . ."

Ariane shook her head. "I don't think we can. I barely managed to get both of us to Hudson Bay. I don't think I can drag much more along."

"One backpack, that's all I'm saying. Lightweight tent, survival blankets, some high-energy bars, matches, flashlight, that kind of thing."

"Well . . ." Ariane paused in thought. "Okay. I think I could manage a single backpack. But I'll have to carry the backpack, not you. It seems . . . it just feels like it will be easier that way."

"I'll make a list and email it to you. You can add anything else you think of." Wally took a deep breath. "What time do you want to go?"

"Let's aim for half past seven. I'll tell Aunt Phyllis we're going to a movie. You come by around six-thirty and we'll pack everything up, then head down to the lake. We can get anywhere we want from there, and it'd be really hard to explain both of us going into the bathroom at the same time —even if we didn't follow it up by disappearing into thin air!"

"OK," Wally said. "Now you really had better get out of here—before Ms. Carson comes back."

He saw Ariane out the front door and then hurried to the garage, where they kept the family camping equipment. He had a lot to do in the next few hours.

Wally Knight, Sidekick to the Lady of the Lake, he thought as he pulled a backpack down from the shelf above the washing machine. He frowned. Somehow "sidekick" didn't sound distinguished enough . . .

He grinned. "Wally Knight," he said out loud. "Companion of the Order of the Lady."

Much better! He unzipped the backpack and started packing.

Twenty minutes after leaving Wally's house, Ariane reached her block. During her walk, she had rehearsed various explanations, trying to figure out what she would put in the note she was going to leave for Aunt Phyllis before she set out with Wally for the "movie." She had no idea when they would be back.

Or *if* they would be back.

She stopped suddenly.

A mud-splattered brown Buick that she didn't recognize was parked in front of her house—and the driver was on the front step . . .

. . . talking to Aunt Phyllis.

There was no mistaking that grey-streaked ponytail: it was the man who had chased her that morning. *How many cars does he have, anyway?*

Ariane didn't know what to do. If she gave in to her instinct to dash up the walk and protect Aunt Phyllis, the ponytailed man would just grab her—and Rex Major would win. Besides, it didn't look like he was threatening her aunt. As far as Ariane could tell, they were just talking.

But . . . about what?

The ponytailed man had his back to her, and if Aunt Phyllis had noticed her, she didn't give any sign of it. Ariane ducked behind the hedge between Aunt Phyllis's house and the one next door and, half-crouched, crept closer.

The neighbour's dry, brown lawn crunched under her feet, and she had to stop farther from the porch than she'd hoped, afraid the ponytailed man would hear the movement in the bushes. Snatches of his words drifted in her direction through the thin screen of red and yellow leaves still clinging to the hedge's dry brown twigs. If she cocked her head just right, she could see the back of his head through a gap in the foliage.

"... principal has instituted ... policy ... following up all suspensions ... concerned by ... attitude not what it should be ..."

"I understand." Aunt Phyllis's voice came through loud and clear; she sounded like an actress projecting to the back row of a theatre. "But it's not my problem anymore."

"I don't understand ... your niece ..." the man's voice disappeared into mumble.

"She's gone," Aunt Phyllis said. "Moved out. She's old enough to live on her own, she said, and off she went. I couldn't stop her. Didn't really want to. She's been nothing but trouble since she got here."

Ariane couldn't believe her ears. Aunt Phyllis was protecting her—but how did she know Ariane *needed* protection?

The man ran his fingers through his hair. "... saw her yesterday ... didn't say anything ..."

"Why should she? She probably doesn't want the school to know where she's gone. She certainly didn't tell me."

"... irregular ... school board must be notified ..."

"Notify away. I've washed my hands of her. It's got nothing more to do with me. Now if you'll excuse me, I have work to do. Good day." And she turned and went into the house, closing the door firmly behind her.

The man stood on the step for a moment. He raised his hand as though intending to knock again, then abruptly turned and strode back down the walk to the waiting Buick. Ariane scurried in closer to the hedge and scrunched down as close to its prickly branches as she could. If he spotted her now . . .

He didn't. He started the Buick and roared down the street. The tires squealed as he ran the stop sign at College and turned left toward downtown.

Ariane straightened up to stare after him.

"I think you and I should have a talk," Aunt Phyllis said from behind her.

❧ 9 ❧

ATTACK OF THE LIZARDOID

THE SHORT WALK to the house seemed to take forever, but it still wasn't long enough to give Ariane time to figure out why her aunt had lied to the ponytailed man. Aunt Phyllis, after looking up and down the street and locking the front door, followed Ariane into the living room. She pointed to the overstuffed armchair in the corner, and Ariane obeyed the unspoken instruction to sit down. Then Aunt Phyllis sat on the couch, took a deep breath, and said, "You've seen the Lady of the Lake, haven't you?"

Everything Ariane had been thinking about saying scurried away like cockroaches caught in the light. She gaped.

Aunt Phyllis sighed. "I've hoped—prayed—this wouldn't happen. I've hoped that our family's curse had skipped a generation. It often does, at least in legends. But it hasn't, has it?"

That broke through Ariane's befuddlement. "My mother saw the Lady of the Lake?" *I was right!*

"So she told me." Aunt Phyllis's expression softened and

her eyes unfocused a little, as though she were looking at something far away. "And so did I . . . almost."

"What?" *That* was so unexpected that it felt to Ariane like she'd been slapped across the face with an ice-filled rubber glove. "You saw the Lady of the Lake?"

"Almost," Aunt Phyllis said. "It happened when I was about your age, and your mother was barely six—about a year before our mother died. We were staying at the family cabin at Emma Lake. I went for a walk along the shore. And I heard . . . singing. Chanting. The water was . . . calling to me. It wanted me to wade into it. I looked out at the lake, and I saw a . . . a swirling in the water, and then it opened up, like a doorway . . ."

She sighed. "And I ran away. I was terrified. Even though I could hear the water's call, I turned my back on it."

Hope kindled in Ariane, hope that she'd found another—completely unexpected—ally. "Did you tell Mom?"

Aunt Phyllis nodded. "I couldn't tell *our* mother, so I told Emily. I told her it was just a story, a fairy tale, but she knew I was lying, that I'd really seen something. Then I tried to lie to myself, tried to convince myself I hadn't really seen anything at all, that I'd imagined it. I kept away from the lake for the rest of our stay, and the next day, we went home. And that was that. Until . . ." She sighed. "Until I got this." She reached inside her apron pocket and pulled out a folded piece of paper. "A letter from Emily . . . mailed from the hospital just before she disappeared."

Ariane's heart skipped a beat and anger heated her cheeks. *"And you've never showed it to me?"*

"It wasn't for you. It was for me. And I didn't want to upset you. It was . . . distressing. I thought it meant your mother really *had* gone crazy, and I didn't want you to think that. *I didn't want to think that.* But when that man showed up on the doorstep twenty minutes ago, asking after you—representing the school, indeed! On a Sunday?—I didn't believe him for one minute. I have a feel for people, you know. I can tell when they're lying. And that's when I realized I have to show you this." She held out the paper. "Read it."

Fingers trembling, Ariane took the letter and unfolded it. She recognized her mother's handwriting, and her eyes blurred. But she blinked away the threatening tears and began to read.

Dear Phyllis,

I have hesitated to write because I don't want to worry you, but now I feel I must. After all, you saw her too . . . the Lady of the Lake. At Emma Lake, the summer before Mom died, remember? You tried to pretend you were just telling a story, but I knew better.

If you ever saw her again, you never told me. And as the years went by I hardly thought of it anymore. Until . . .

Phyllis, I saw her. I talked to her. Not at Emma Lake, but right here in Regina, in Wascana Lake. I went for a walk around the lake, same as I've done a thousand times, but this time . . . I heard singing. I heard the water calling to me. I went down to the shore, and I saw an opening in the water, like a trapdoor, with steps, leading down . . . just like you told me about all those years ago.

And the singing . . . I wish I could describe it to you. It was breathtaking. It pulled at me. I couldn't resist it. I don't know how you did. I went down the steps, into a kind of throne room under the water, and there was a woman . . . a woman made of water. She talked to me. She told me she was the Lady of the Lake, from the days of King Arthur, and that I had to help her retrieve the shards of Excalibur from their hiding places all over the world, and re-forge the sword before Merlin could claim it. She said Rex Major, the computer guy, is really Merlin, but I could defeat him with the power of the Lady of the Lake, that all I had to do was accept it, and I would have all the power I needed . . .

But . . . it was all too strange. I didn't listen anymore. "I don't want your power!" I told her. "I reject it!"

And then she grew angry. "Reject it? Without it, you are helpless," she told me. "Rex Major will be able to find you. Though you reject my power, a portion of it will still cling to you for a time. He will use it to track you down. He will track down your daughter. She, too, is my heir. If you reject the power I offer, you are defenceless against him."

"I don't want your power!" I screamed at her again. "I just want my normal life!" And then I turned and ran.

The water closed in on me, almost drowned me. I stumbled home, half-drowned, freezing, and Ariane called 911

That paragraph broke off in mid-sentence, as though Ariane's mother had thought better of what she was about to write. Ariane continued reading.

I have to go away. I have to. Before Merlin—Rex Major—
finds out who I am, finds out I have a daughter . . . or a
sister.

I know this sounds crazy. I'm just asking you, Phyl, to
be careful. Be on the lookout for strange men asking
strange questions. And . . . take care of my little girl. Don't
tell her anything about this. She already thinks I've gone
crazy. This would just confirm it.

Goodbye, Phyl. I don't think we'll see each other again.
I love you.

Emily

Ariane gulped air. "She ran away to protect me."

Aunt Phyllis nodded. "As she saw it, it was the only thing to do."

"Did you show this letter to the police?"

Aunt Phyllis shook her head. "It makes her sound crazy. And I actually thought she *was*, when I read it for the first time while I was in hospital for my first surgery. I mean . . . Rex Major is really Merlin? And he's searching for the shards of Excalibur? I thought she had just taken the story I told her when we were kids, a story about something I'd convinced *myself* never really happened, and she'd woven it into her delusion." She folded the letter and slipped it back into her flowered apron. "But then . . ." She stopped and took another deep breath. "Last week . . . the night after the school told me you were suspended . . . I had a dream." Her voice dropped to a whisper. "I saw the Lady, a woman all in white, in Emma Lake, right where I heard the singing so many years ago. She rose to the surface, her face broke the water, and she said, 'Beware of Merlin. He is searching for you . . . and he knows I have visited Ariane.' And then she melted away." Aunt Phyllis raised her eyes and looked at Ariane steadily. "She came to you, didn't she? And spoke to you? Just like she did to your mother. But unlike your mother —you didn't run away. You accepted the power."

Ariane wanted to deny it. Somehow, having all this move into the humdrum reality of her life seemed *wrong*, against the rules she had absorbed from years of reading children's fantasy stories. The parents or guardians of the kids involved never knew what was really going on.

But this wasn't a story. This was reality. And Aunt Phyllis deserved the truth.

As simply as she could, Ariane told Aunt Phyllis everything that had happened since she had seen the staircase leading into the waters of Wascana Lake.

Aunt Phyllis listened intently, her eyes fixed on Ariane's. She seemed perfectly calm, but her face grew paler and paler, and when Ariane glanced down, she saw Aunt Phyllis's fingers digging into the flowered upholstery of the couch. "And so, tonight . . . we're going," Ariane finished. "Wally and me. To the Northwest Territories. By . . ." She hesitated, but had to say it. "By magic." She searched Aunt Phyllis's face. "Do you think I'm crazy?"

A small smile lifted the corners of Aunt Phyllis's mouth. "If you are, then I was, too, all those years ago—and I still am. I've heard of shared delusions, but not spread out among three people—four, counting Wally—over decades." Her smile faded. "What I want is for the whole thing to go away. Why should *you* be saddled with saving the world?"

"I don't know," Ariane said. "It's like . . . an inherited disease or something. I don't seem to have any choice."

Aunt Phyllis snorted. "An inherited disease. That's it, isn't it? We inherited . . . something. The ability to use the power of the Lady of the Lake. It's like the old saying, 'You can choose your friends, but you can't choose your family.' Especially not your family from a millennium and a half ago." She looked down at her twisting fingers, and clenched them tightly in the afghan. "How can I let you go, Ariane?" she said softly. "You're all I have left of Emily, all I have left of a family. If anything happens to you . . ."

"But staying here isn't safe, either, Aunt Phyllis," Ariane said. "Rex Major knows who I am. He knows where I live. By now, he must know you're my guardian. If he decides to simply kidnap me . . . there won't be anything we can do to stop him." *There might be something* I *can do*, she thought, remembering the power she had been able to unleash against Flish and the coven—but she had no idea if that would work on Merlin himself. And she didn't want to sit around to find out. "If I go up north, if I can actually get this first shard of Excalibur, then at least I'm fighting back. And after that . . ."

"After that, what, Ariane?" Aunt Phyllis said. "Rex Major will still know where you live. He'll still be able to snatch you away without warning. Where do we go? How do we escape one of the richest men in the world?"

Ariane shook her head. "I don't know, Aunt Phyllis. But the Lady of the Lake hasn't given us any choice. We have to try to defeat him. We have to."

"*Damn* the Lady of the Lake!" Aunt Phyllis said, and Ariane stared at her. Her aunt had never sworn in front of her before. "What gives her the right to get our family mixed up in some battle that goes back more than a thousand years?" She glared at Ariane as though expecting her to defend the Lady, but Ariane agreed with her.

Oh, do you? a part of her wondered. *Or are you secretly glad? The power . . . you like having it, don't you?*

I don't know, she answered herself. *I don't know anything.*

Either way, she remained silent—and Aunt Phyllis remained angry. Ariane could see it in the bright red splotches on her cheeks and the flaring of her nostrils. But she spoke with forced, icy calmness. "But I guess you're right, Ariane. She hasn't left us any choice. She's fixed our course for us, right into the heart of the storm, and the best we can do is batten down the hatches and hope to ride it out. And if I ever meet her outside of a dream, I'll—" She stopped, clenched her jaw for a moment, then gave a sharp, short nod. "Very well, then. You and Wally have to go to the Northwest Territories, by magic, to retrieve the first shard of Excalibur." She paused. "I still don't really understand how Wally got involved in all of this. You two really aren't . . .?"

Ariane felt her face flush. "No!"

"OK, OK." Aunt Phyllis held up her hands. "Well, I'm glad someone is going with you, at least. Though he's not exactly a knight in shining armour, at least he's a Knight."

Ariane rolled her eyes. "Aunt Phyllis!"

Her aunt chuckled, but her amusement died quickly. "How can I help? What do you need to take with you? Food? Supplies?"

"I don't think I can transport much more than Wally, and whatever we are already carrying," Ariane said. "So we can't take a lot. But food—yeah, food would be good. We'll have to put it in something waterproof, though."

"I can do that. Crackers, cheese, summer sausage, beef jerky, chocolate, nuts. Lightweight but lots of calories." Aunt Phyllis stood. "Let's get at it."

Ariane jumped up. "Wait a minute."

Aunt Phyllis paused. "What?"

"What about you?"

"What about me?"

"What will you do if Major's . . . uh, 'henchman' . . . comes back?" Ariane felt a little silly. She'd never used the word "henchman" in a sentence before. "What if he decides to kidnap *you* instead of *me*?"

Aunt Phyllis smiled a strange little smile Ariane had never seen before. "You leave Major's 'henchman' to me."

The next couple of hours passed by in a blur. Ariane went upstairs and discovered that Wally had indeed emailed her a list of supplies—a rather daunting one. Ariane wondered how he planned to fit it all into a backpack, whether she'd be able to stand up once she put it on—and most importantly, whether she had the energy to transport it as far as they had to go.

Wally had highlighted several items on the list he didn't think he had in his house, such as spare flashlight batteries. For once, Aunt Phyllis's habit of imagining possible disasters came in handy. She had several basement shelves filled with emergency supplies—including waterproof bags into which she stuffed the food. With her help, Ariane soon filled in the gaps in Wally's list. Pendragon sat on the basement steps, tail curled neatly around his toes, watching her pack with wide green eyes.

Wally showed up in person promptly at six-thirty. "Hello, Ms. Forsythe," he said to Aunt Phyllis. "I sure am looking forward to seeing a movie with Ariane this evening." He sounded like a bad actor in a high school play.

Aunt Phyllis caught Ariane's eye and winked, then gave Wally an innocent-looking smile. "What movie are you going to see? *Camelot?*" The smile widened. "*Excalibur?*"

Wally's mouth fell open, and Aunt Phyllis chuckled as she patted his arm. "Ariane has told me everything. So you don't have to worry about pretending."

"Every—" Wally's gaze slid past Aunt Phyllis to Ariane, "—thing?"

"Everything," Ariane confirmed with a grin. "And Aunt Phyllis has been helping me round up supplies. Come upstairs and help me pack, and I'll tell you all about it."

The pile of stuff on the bed looked impossibly huge, but it took up far less space when organized in the backpack. In the end the only things left behind were a small axe and some cooking utensils.

"We're not really planning to camp," Ariane pointed out. "And we've got knives."

"You can't chop branches to build a lean-to with a knife," Wally warned. "And just because we're not planning to camp doesn't mean we won't end up camping."

"The axe is too heavy. It stays behind." Ariane hefted the backpack, slipped it on, and staggered backward a step or two before she caught her balance. "I don't know if I can get even this much all the way to the Northwest Territories. And we haven't added the food yet!"

"Well, don't wear it now! Save your strength until we're ready to go." Wally looked around the room, hesitated. "*Are we ready to go?*"

"There's one thing we're missing," Ariane said. "We don't have a clue as to the layout of the mine."

"Hmmm," Wally said. "Well, let's take a look . . ."

He sat down at the computer.

WALLY PRIDED himself on his online-researching skills. If there was information about a topic to be found on the Web, he was confident he could find it. And something like a diamond mine in the Northwest Territories should be easy. Big corporations loved to promote their projects, especially flashy ones, and what could be flashier than a diamond mine?

For a moment he hesitated, remembering the threatening warning they had received from Rex Major's henchman the previous evening. But they'd used the computer again after that with no problem. *Besides*, Wally thought. *I've seen scarier things than that in video games.*

He twitched the mouse to bring the hibernating computer to life, and the monitor lit up. "We probably can't get a detailed map, but the mining company is bound to have a website. If nothing else, there ought to be photos of the place."

"Worth a try." Ariane sat on the edge of the bed to watch Wally work.

Wally opened the browser, typed "Thunderhill Diamond Mine" into the search field in the upper-right corner, and hit RETURN.

The first entry was the mine's own website. "Jackpot," he said, perversely annoyed that he hadn't had the chance to show off his "skillz." He clicked on the link, and the screen lit up with a picture of buildings, taken from the other side of a large lake. Only a few low plants, poking up between the big boulders scattered around, kept the surrounding countryside from being completely barren. "North of the tree line," Wally said, feeling sheepish. "Guess you were right to leave out the axe."

Ariane very politely did not say, "I told you so."

Wally kept scrolling. After a moment, he whistled. "Look at this!" He pointed to the screen. "At any given time, there are seven hundred people working in the mine. Seven hundred! That's bigger than half the towns in Saskatchewan." He leaned closer to view the fine print. "It's got a gym, squash and racquetball courts, a games room, a theatre, TV lounges, high-speed Internet access, satellite telephones, private rooms and private bathrooms for everyone, a gourmet chef . . ." He leaned back and shook his head. "It's not a diamond mine, it's a resort!"

"It's also only two hundred kilometres south of the Arctic Circle in the middle of the treeless tundra and a six-hour drive from the nearest town—if it's winter, which is the only time there's a road," Ariane pointed out, reading over his shoulder. "Some resort."

"Well, maybe not in winter," Wally conceded. "But in the summer, I'm telling you, they could make as much money renting out rooms as they do mining diamonds."

He scrolled further. "Ah! There's a brochure called 'All About Thunderhill.' Let's try that." He clicked again, and two seconds later they were looking at a map of the mine. "Not very detailed," Wally said, "but a lot better than nothing!" He clicked PRINT. The inkjet printer to the left of the monitor hummed to life.

Wally was about to get up to grab the printout when the monitor flickered and turned a brilliant, poisonous green. He blinked and leaned forward. "I think your video card is screwed . . . no, wait a minute, I can see something in there. Maybe it's a video file that—"

His voice and his breath both choked off: a green, clawed hand, covered in scales, burst from the surface of the monitor and seized him by the throat. He scrabbled at it, trying to pry it off, but his fingers slid uselessly off scales as hard and impervious as glass. The hand began to squeeze . . . he couldn't breathe . . .

Out of the corner of his eye he saw a horrified Ariane leap for the wall socket. She jerked out the power bar plug. The printer stuttered to a halt, the disk drive stopped in mid-chatter, but the green-scaled hand didn't falter, and the algae-green glow of the monitor didn't so much as flicker.

Wally, dizzy and terrified, was afraid the hand would drag him into the poisonous green soup the monitor's surface had become, but instead it pushed him back, away from the computer. The wheels of Ariane's ancient office desk chair squeaked horribly as they rolled centimetre by centimetre away from the desk—and slowly, the arm attached to that scaly green hand appeared. An armour-plated elbow came through next, then a massive green bicep . . .

. . . which meant the head and the rest of the body couldn't be too far behind. Wally did *not* want to see either . . . but then, it seemed likely he wouldn't be seeing anything at all in a minute. His vision had narrowed to a blurred tunnel.

He couldn't feel his arms and legs. A buzzing filled his head . . .

Think . . . think! The thing was coming out of the computer, so it had to be connected to it somehow. But the computer was not only off, it was unplugged . . .

Unplugged from the wall socket, but not from the Internet! A blue Ethernet cable ran from the back of the computer to the DSL modem, and a grey cable attached the modem to an outlet in the wall. Wally quit trying to pry the fingers from his neck and instead grabbed Ariane's arm. She turned wide eyes to him, and he pointed weakly at the high-speed cables. Then he had to turn away and grip the scaly arm again as it lifted him completely off the floor. Ariane dropped to her hands and knees and fell out of his sight. He hoped desperately she had understood. His legs kicked uncontrollably in mid-air. One flailing foot sent the desk chair rolling across the floor. He heard it crash against something. His tunnel of vision was shrinking. All he could see were spots of grey and green light . . .

And then the floor whacked against Wally's knees as he crashed onto it, gasping, pulling in huge, shuddering gulps of precious air through a throat as raw as freshly ground beef but no longer in the grip of a giant lizard. His vision flooded back, the buzzing in his ears subsided, and he raised a shaking hand to his sore neck.

Ariane crawled into sight, and he managed a small smile. "Worst computer virus I ever saw." Talking made him cough. His hand felt sticky. He pulled it away from his throat and saw it was smeared with blood. "I'm bleeding!"

"Let me see." Ariane put her hand in his hair and tilted his head back to examine his throat. "It's not serious," she assured him after a moment. She let go of his head. "Just a couple of little claw punctures. No worse than shaving cuts."

Wally laughed shakily. "I wouldn't know."

Ariane grinned, revealing teeth only slightly whiter than her face. "Anyway, you'll live."

This time, Wally thought.

He sat up, groaning. Ariane helped him to his feet, then grabbed a handful of tissues from a box by her bed and held them out to him. He dabbed at the punctures on his neck. "I'm lucky he didn't just rip my throat out."

"He was using you to pull himself out of the computer. If he'd made it . . ."

". . . we'd both be lizard chow."

Ariane frowned. "But Major doesn't want to kill me."

"That's just guesswork on our part. Don't go thinking you're invulnerable." He dabbed at the cuts again. "Besides, who says that thing would have killed you? It might have just dragged you back into . . . wherever it came from."

"It could have killed *you*, though." She bit her lip. "Wally, you should—"

"Don't tell me what I should do," Wally snapped. "I can make my own decisions. And I've decided to help you." *No matter what the cost?* a small voice asked, but he did his best to ignore it. He held out the bloody tissues. "I think I need some more."

"You'd better come into the bathroom. We'll put some antiseptic and then some band-aids on those wounds. Who knows what kind of germs a Lizardoid—" Ariane stopped. "That's what it was! I thought it looked familiar. It was a Lizardoid!"

Wally blinked. "You mean like in *Devil Swamp*?"

"*Exactly* like it. I was playing it just a few days ago." She looked at the unpowered, unplugged computer. Its blank monitor looked back innocently. "Last time Major just used the computer to send us a warning. This time he turned a *computer* monster into a *real* one." She gave Wally a bleak look. "We're going to have to be very careful using computers from now on."

"Now *that* hurts," Wally muttered.

Ariane laughed. "Let's get you into the bathroom."

She had just put a band-aid on the last puncture when Aunt Phyllis appeared at the bathroom door. For some reason, she was carrying a baseball bat.

"What happened?" Aunt Phyllis looked at Wally's neck, and then at Ariane. "Never mind, there's no time. You'd better go *now*. A car just pulled up outside."

NORTH. NORTH. NORTH!

Ariane's heartbeat shifted into high gear. "He knows where I am. We're idiots for using the computer!"

"No kidding." Wally massaged his throat. "Are we ready?"

No, Ariane thought. Out loud she said, "Ready as we'll ever be. We've packed everything." She slung the pack onto her shoulders. "Oof. Including the kitchen sink, it feels like."

"Not quite everything!" Wally dashed into the bedroom and grabbed the sheets of paper protruding from the mouth of the printer. He flipped through them. "Looks like we got it all except the last page. We got the map, anyway."

Aunt Phyllis pointed at the backpack. "Will you be able to . . . um . . . 'move' all that?"

"I think so." *I hope so.*

"Then go. I don't know what our friend outside has planned, but he could be breaking down the door any minute now."

"We can't leave you—"

Aunt Phyllis cut her off. "Go!" She lifted the baseball bat, expression fierce. "I told you, leave him to me."

It didn't feel right, but they had no choice. "Be careful," Ariane said, then surprised Aunt Phyllis—and herself—by flinging her arms around her. "Don't take any chances."

Aunt Phyllis squeezed her tightly with her one free arm. "Look who's talking." She pushed Ariane away. "Now go. Go!" She hesitated. "Um . . . how *do* you go, exactly?"

Ariane laughed. She suddenly felt giddy with excitement and eagerness. It felt like . . . like the day she had finally mustered the courage to dive off the high board at the swimming pool. "We start by going to the bathroom."

Wally and Aunt Phyllis both laughed. Once in the bathroom, Ariane started the tap. Her heart pounded, and when she reached out and took Wally's hand, she felt his pulse racing too. "Goodbye, Aunt Phyllis. I don't know how long this will take—"

"However long it takes, take it," Aunt Phyllis said.

Wally blinked. "I just thought of something. When I don't come home tonight, Ms. Carson will—"

"Leave her to me," Aunt Phyllis said. "I'll tell her you're staying here overnight—and not to worry, I'm chaperoning. And I'll make your excuses to the school tomorrow too. I can cover you for one day, anyway. Now, both of you, *go!* Just . . . be safe."

"I promise," Ariane said, though they both knew it was a promise she couldn't keep. She put her free hand into the stream of water falling from the tap, paused a moment to listen for the water's call, and then . . .

Plunged.

The water embraced her instantly and warmly, but she

could feel it resisting Wally and the backpack. Her power poured out and overcame that resistance. She couldn't keep it up for long. But this time, unlike last time, she knew exactly where she wanted to go. Keeping her mind fiercely focused, she raced north, through pipes and ponds, rivers and rapids, creeks and cataracts, toward the shard of Excalibur.

North. North. *North!*

Though she had no way to measure time, the journey seemed to be taking far longer than the trip to Hudson Bay. Wally and the backpack dragged at her, and Ariane began to fear that the duration of the journey would exceed the limits of her power.

All the time, the song of the sword sang in her head. She could almost *see* the shard, burning in her mind like a fiery beacon, but no matter how hard she tried, she couldn't reach it. It seemed to be in a tightly enclosed space, too small to accommodate them. All she could do was get as close to it as possible, and hope that was close enough. With the last strength remaining in her, she found a body of water that would serve, and released the magic.

Water geysered as they materialized. With her power depleted, the cold lashed around her body and limbs like steel cables squeezing out her breath, and belatedly she realized their simple, deadly mistake:

She couldn't swim wearing a backpack.

It pulled her under like an anchor tied to her back. She clutched instinctively at Wally's wrist, even as she remembered that he couldn't swim and she would pull him down with her. But he was holding her up somehow. Amazed, she quit struggling . . . and found that her feet touched bottom.

Feeling more than a little foolish, she straightened up, and her head broke into the open air.

The clouds glowed a sickly grey-orange, reflecting dozens of sodium-vapour lights hung on posts and buildings at least half a mile beyond the far shore of the large pond in which they'd materialized. The cloud-light cast a ghostly pallor across the snow-covered ground. Somewhere out of sight, machinery growled and grumbled like restless dragons.

Ariane wrapped her arms around her shivering body and splashed toward the shore. "We've g-got to g-get warm!"

WALLY SPLASHED onto the icy shore just ahead of Ariane, his teeth chattering so hard he thought the enamel would crack. Having to materialize in water really sucked. Especially for someone like him, who swam about as well as a rock. And especially when the first shard was in the Northwest Territories. Why couldn't it have been in Florida?

At least it was warm for the Northwest Territories: right around freezing, he guessed. Otherwise they might have materialized under ice too thick to break through. He shuddered (or shivered, it was hard to tell the difference) at the thought.

Still, even if their clothes weren't freezing solid in the wind, it was plenty cold enough for him to sense Old Man Hypothermia lurking just around the corner. "C-can't you w-wish the w-water off of us, l-like you d-did last t-time?"

Ariane had collapsed on the ground, head down, and didn't even look up. "C-can't," she said dully. "I'm u-used up. N-nothing left."

"G-guess we do this the old-f-fashioned way, th-then." With clumsy fingers, Wally helped Ariane take off the backpack, opened it up, and started pulling out supplies.

Everything was dry—the waterproof bags and backpack had seen to that. The tiny two-person pop-open tent went up without a hitch, and he had the space heater with its frighteningly small tank of propane running in moments. Wally stood outside the tent and froze for an agonizing additional five minutes while Ariane put on dry clothes, then it was his turn to strip and struggle into dry things while she waited outside. Shortly after that, though, they were both snug in their super-lightweight fold-to-next-to-nothing "space-blanket" sleeping bags. They sat quietly, warming up and munching on high-protein hiking bars.

Wally licked the last crumbs of his bar off his fingers and crumpled the wrapper. "So far, so good. But what happens next? Do we try to find the shard tonight?"

There was no reply. He glanced over at the other sleeping bag. Ariane had slumped over onto her side, eyes closed. Her mouth hung slightly open and something very close to a snore issued from it.

I guess that answers that. Wally grinned. *Wally's Second Law of Sidekickery: Sleep when the heroine sleeps.*

If he could. Wally had learned tricks like making a fire and what to eat in the forest in his Outdoor Education class, but so far, they'd only made day trips, never slept outdoors. And for the Knights, "camping" meant a trip in the big silver motor home tucked away in the third bay of the garage. The thin floor of the tent wasn't exactly the air mattress he was used to on those trips, and the ground felt hard as . . . well, as frozen ground, though the layer of snow helped cushion it some. *Well, it's just as well if I don't sleep. Someone should probably keep watch . . . just in case.*

He lay back in his own sleeping bag, hands behind his head, resigning himself to a sleepless night.

He woke inside a tent aglow in sunlight, just as the flap was flung wide from outside.

"All right," a man's voice said gruffly. "Come out where we can see you."

From somewhere nearby came the roar of a low-flying airplane.

A PAIR OF LOVEBIRDS

Rex Major gazed avidly out the window as the Twin
Otter circled the Thunderhill Diamond Mine on a bright
Monday morning. The blizzard had carried on through most
of Sunday, but had finally blown itself out shortly after
sunset. Over the engine noise, he only heard snatches of
Ursu's tour-guide patter from the seat beside him. "The
largest building is the process plant . . . runs twenty-four
hours a day, three hundred and sixty-five days a year. That's
the main power station . . . diesel engines . . . exhaust heat
recovered to heat buildings. And we call that the utilidor: it's
a covered walkway so workers don't have to go outside
during bad weather. The ore stockpile there lets us keep
working even if regular ore supplies are interrupted . . .
ammonium nitrate storage plant over there. We use ANFO
—ammonium nitrate and fuel oil—for blasting . . ."

He went on, but Major tuned him out. He still didn't
know exactly where the shard of Excalibur was hidden, but
it was down there somewhere—he could feel it, a glimmering

sliver of the power of Faerie that had once been his and would be again.

A blue blotch on the far side of the small lake south of the mine drew his attention. A yellow pickup truck had pulled up not far from it and he could see four men approaching it on foot.

"What's going on there?" he said, interrupting Ursu's glowing account of the workings of the mine's environmentally friendly sewage treatment and disposal system.

Ursu leaned over him to get a better look. "Probably hunters. We get them from time to time. Security is on it."

The pilot's voice came on the intercom. "Making our final approach now, gentlemen. I hope you enjoyed your flight!"

Major stared at the tent. Something about it bothered him, but he couldn't figure out why. He put it out of his mind and settled back into his seat. Excalibur, or at least the first precious shard of it, was waiting for him.

As long as they didn't crash on landing.

Stupid way to fly, he thought for the umpteenth time, gripping the arms of the chair as the air got bumpier closer to the ground. *Give me magic any time.*

ARIANE, coatless, stood shivering in the snow beside Wally, facing the three men who had woken them up so abruptly. In the distance, the sound of the airplane engine changed pitch and then died away as the plane came in for a landing. Ariane wondered if Rex Major himself might be on that plane, arriving for his tour of the mine, but she didn't take her attention off the three men. Each was armed with a pistol in a black leather holster, and two of them, standing next to a bright yellow pickup truck with an extended cab, also held rifles. Each wore a heavy blue uniform jacket with the Thunderhill Diamonds logo stitched over one breast pocket and a name over the other. Black letters on white armbands read SECURITY.

"Anyone else in there?" said the man who had opened the tent flap. DREZNER, Ariane read on his jacket. He looked tall enough to play in the NBA and broad enough to be a professional wrestler.

"N-no," said Wally. "There's just us." With his head tousled and a big red mark on his left cheek from a wrinkle he'd slept on, he looked even younger than usual.

"I'll take a look anyway, if you don't mind." Drezner's tone made it clear he didn't care if they minded or not.

Ariane and Wally stepped aside. The other three men kept a close watch on them while Drezner went inside the tent. They could hear him rummaging through their things. After a moment he came out again, carrying their coats in one hand and the backpack in the other. He put the backpack on the ground and held out the coats. As they gratefully pulled them on, he said, "All right, what are you two kids doing here? This is private property."

"We didn't see any signs," Ariane said truthfully. "We're just . . . passing by."

"You don't have enough supplies to be 'passing by.' We're a hundred kilometres from the nearest village." Drezner put his hands on his hips. "How did you get here?"

Something in the man's tone reminded Ariane of Mr. Stanton, the vice principal. She could feel her temper rising, but she held it down, refusing to give in to the temptation to say, "We swam." Instead, she said nothing.

Wally wasn't as reticent. "What does it matter? We're just a couple of kids. You said so yourself. Surely you don't think we're here to try to steal your diamonds."

Drezner gave him a sharp look. Ariane winced. *I don't think that helped, Wally.* She wished the Lady's power included telepathy. Since it didn't, she had to make do with a frown in Wally's direction. He gave no sign he had seen it.

"You don't look like a threat," Drezner said. "But whoever brought you here could be—and you couldn't possibly have gotten here on your own. Maybe you're just here to divert our attention from something happening somewhere else. So we'll be detaining you until we figure it out."

"You've got no right to detain us!" Wally said. "We haven't done anything!"

Not yet, Ariane thought. She glanced over her shoulder, hoping to catch a glimpse of the airplane they had heard. But the airstrip was out of sight on the other side of a low ridge. A road ran down from the ridge and past the east side of the lake to the main compound.

Drezner followed her gaze and frowned. He pulled a walkie-talkie from his belt. "Security Five to Security One. Smitty, is everything OK at the airstrip? Over."

"Everything's fine, Drez," a voice crackled. "Mr. Ursu and Rex Major just landed. Why do you ask? Over."

"Got a couple of trespassers," Drezner said, his eyes never leaving Ariane's face. "Looks like a pair of teen lovebirds—" Ariane blushed, and Wally turned bright red—"but you never know. Keep me posted. Security Five, over and out." He hooked the walkie-talkie back onto his belt.

"Awfully big coincidence, you two turning up just when we've got a VIP visitor."

Ariane kept silent, but Wally heaved an exaggerated sigh. "Drez—can I call you Drez?"

"No," Drezner said.

Wally barely hesitated. "OK. Well, uh . . . sir . . . we're not, uh, 'lovebirds'—may I just say, 'Yuck!'—she's my sister."

Yuck? Ariane thought with a touch of indignation.

Wally waved one hand in a vaguely westerly direction. "Our folks are camping over there a . . . a ways. We just . . . snuck off. For fun. We planned to be back in time for breakfast. But we overslept." His voice gained confidence as his story developed. "Thank goodness you woke us up! They're going to be awfully worried about us, aren't they, sis?"

Ariane nodded. "Awfully worried."

Drezner glanced to the west. "Over there 'a ways,' huh?"

"Yes, sir." Wally nodded.

"And you 'snuck off.' For 'fun.'"

"Yes, sir."

"In the middle of a blizzard? Because until about seven o'clock last night, you could barely see your hand in front of your face out here."

Wally opened his mouth, then closed it again.

Oops, Ariane thought.

"Right." Drezner unhooked his walkie-talkie again. "Security Five to HQ. Over."

"HQ here. What's up, Drez? Over."

"Bill, our trespassers are a couple of kids. They claim they sneaked out of their parents' camp somewhere west of here last night."

"Last night?" The voice on the other end sounded skeptical. "In that weather?"

"That's what they say." Drezner watched Wally as he spoke. "Can we send the chopper up, check it out? If they're telling the truth, their parents will be worried about them. Over."

"Sure thing. I think Carl is on standby . . . yeah. I'll have him in the air in fifteen minutes. Over."

"Great. Over and out." Drezner hung the walkie-talkie back on his belt.

"Thanks a lot!" Wally said. He'd obviously decided it was too late to back down from his story now. "You shouldn't have any trouble finding them—we can't be more than five kilometres from the campsite."

"Uh huh." Drezner did not sound convinced. "Well, until we do, you're going to be our guests." He turned his head. "Vasili, Tom, get the tent into the back." The two guards by the truck slung their rifles over their shoulders and came forward. As they took down the tent with quick efficiency, Drezner put one heavy hand on Ariane's shoulder and the other on Wally's, and propelled them toward the truck. Ariane snatched up their backpack as they passed it. They waited by the vehicle until the tent had been loaded aboard, then Wally was placed in the front seat, between Drezner and "Vasili" (his name tag read MARAGOS), while Ariane got the back seat, directly behind Drezner and next to "Tom" (POITRAS).

As Ariane climbed in, Drezner reached out and lifted Wally's chin, revealing the band-aids she had put on his throat after the attack of the Lizardoid the night before. "What happened to your neck?" Drezner said.

"Shaving cuts," Wally said. He rubbed his throat. "Tough beard. You know how it is."

Drezner snorted and turned the key to start the engine.

As the truck rolled toward the buildings whose lights they had seen the night before, Ariane dug in the pockets of the backpack for a couple of granola bars, passing one to Wally before opening her own and munching on it as they drove. She needed energy, and it looked like a proper breakfast was out of the question.

As they approached the road east of the lake, they slowed to let two other pickups zip past in a cloud of snow. Wally turned to look at Ariane, and she could read the question in his eyes. *Rex Major?*

But Ariane couldn't confirm either way. *And what difference does it make anyway?* Gloom gripped her. It wouldn't take the helicopter pilot long to discover that no one was camped west of the diamond mine. Then there would be questions they couldn't answer, a flight back to Yellowknife to talk to the Mounties, and who knew what after that. Even if they didn't say anything, the Mounties would figure out who they were and trace them back to Regina. An eternity of questions, probably news stories, and a media frenzy would follow . . .

And in the meantime, Rex Major would have the first shard of Excalibur, and would already be looking for the next one.

They continued across a bridge over a rock-strewn stream, then turned left. Their pickup and the two that came from the airfield all stopped at about the same time in front of a two-story building covered in blue-green metal siding. Above a large porch enclosed in glass, big red letters proclaimed, WELCOME TO THE THUNDERHILL DIAMOND MINE.

With Drezner's massive shoulders blocking her view, Ariane couldn't see the other two pickups, but apparently Wally could. He stiffened, then shot her a quick look and jerked his head toward the building. *Rex Major, I presume,* she thought.

By the time she and Wally climbed out of their truck, everyone else had gone inside. Ariane could hear the throbbing sound of a helicopter warming up. She looked around helplessly. Even if she and Wally could outrun Drezner, Maragos and Poitras—*fat chance!*—there was nowhere to hide, not even a corner to dash around. The building stretched dozens of metres in both directions. And so she and Wally meekly followed Drezner up the steps, through a door onto the porch, and then through another door into a hallway.

A sign above a shuttered counter to their left read LUGGAGE PICKUP. Just past it, an open door led to what looked like a waiting room. Just past *that*, a very bored-looking security guard sat inside a theatre-box-office-like glass booth labelled RECEPTION, reading a tattered copy of *Sports Illustrated.* He glanced up when they came in, but then went back to the magazine.

From around the corner at the end of the hall came a snatch of conversation, ". . . dormitories can house more than six hundred workers . . ."

Major must be getting the grand tour, Ariane thought. *At least that will keep him from looking for the shard right away.*

Not that that helped, as long as she was . . .

Her gaze fell on two doors at the end of the hallway,

doors with metal push plates instead of door handles, one with the outline of a man on it, the other with the outline of a woman . . .

"I need to go to the washroom," she said. Wally gave her a sharp look, but she ignored him. "I *really* need to go."

Drezner sighed. "All right. But be quick." He turned to the other guards. "Vasili, you wait outside the door for her. Bring her to HQ when she's done. Tom, you can go back to your regular rounds. You," he said to Wally, "come with me."

Poitras nodded and went back outside. As the door opened and closed, Ariane heard a helicopter chop-chop-chop overhead, presumably heading out to find their ficti-tious parents' camp.

Drezner, Maragos, Wally and Ariane walked down the hall, past doors leading to a lunchroom on their right and something called the Visitor Orientation Centre on their left. Ariane ducked into the ladies' washroom, avoiding Wally's gaze. She was afraid the men would figure out she was up to something if she and Wally even looked at each other.

She went into a stall to take care of urgent business, collecting her wits and her breath in the process. She had to get away from Drezner. *Wally* . . .

Wally will just have to look after himself. She tried not to feel guilty about it. *It's not as if they're going to hurt him.*

The toilet flushed automatically as she left the stall. *They'll hear that,* she thought. *It won't take them long to get suspicious . . .*

She went to the sink and turned on the water, immedi-ately hearing its siren call. Glad she'd eaten the granola bar, she took a deep breath, plunged her hands into it, and let it take her.

She didn't want to go far this time, just far enough to escape the security guards and get as close as possible to the shard of Excalibur. But at first she had no choice at all: the water flowed into the sewer pipe, and from there to the sewage treatment plant. She rushed in her disembodied form through its settlement tanks and filters and evaporators, and hurried along with the treated water down a long pipeline to a lake, but she was getting farther from the shard of Excalibur, not closer to it.

On she hurried, down to the bottom of the lake, down to where water seeped through stone, down to caverns and cavities filled with icy black water that never saw the light of day. That didn't matter though—she was travelling not by light but by feel, reaching out for tendrils of water that would lead her where she needed to go.

It didn't seem to matter how tiny the opening—if water could find its way through, it would, and so could she. But it took energy, so much energy, and if she ran out of energy before she fought her way to the surface . . .

Would she be crushed? Entombed? Blown apart? She didn't know, but she instinctively felt it would be bad.

Very bad.

The shard of Excalibur sang in her mind, urgent, insistent, and closer than it had ever been before. She wanted it with all her heart. But her strength was failing. She needed to find a large body of water . . .

There. Like a dolphin leaping above the waves to seize a breath of air, she burst into the pool she had found and let herself materialize.

She found herself lying flat on her back in the icy

embrace of three feet of dirty water. Shivering, she sat up and looked around.

The terraced, cliff-like walls of an enormous open-pit mine rose all around her, the nearest only four or five metres away. A tendril of water dribbled down it into the pool in which she sat. It amazed and terrified her to think that a moment before she had been part of that tiny stream, had somehow brought her material body in immaterial form through a crack in the wall barely wide enough to slip a dime into. Living in a world where magic was real was bad enough. Living in a world in which magic was not only real, but at her command, was definitely going to take some getting used to.

She put a hand to her head, wincing. The shard of Excalibur sang in her mind with painful intensity. But where was it?

The floor of the mine was a jumbled mess of ice-and-water-filled pits and man-high, snow-shrouded piles of rock. Rutted tracks wound among them. In various places, bulldozers scraped at the ground, shoving rocks and dirt into heaps, apparently at random, though there must have been some pattern to their work that she didn't grasp. At the pit's centre, a giant mechanical shovel methodically dug, taking huge bites of gravel that it then dumped into a waiting truck at the head of a line of similar trucks. As one truck filled, it drove up and out of the pit. At the same time, an empty truck, descending into the pit, joined the back of the line.

For a dizzying moment Ariane couldn't make sense of the scale of things—the machinery looked like toys playing in the sand a dozen metres off. Then she saw someone walking past one of the truck's wheels, which rose well over his head, and everything snapped into place. The shovel was at least two hundred metres away, and the far side of the pit two hundred metres or more beyond that.

She scrambled out of the pool and hid behind a nearby pile of rocks. No one seemed to have noticed her yet, but they would if she sat around like a lump. She ordered the water away from her body and immediately felt warmer.

Now what? she asked herself.

Find the shard, she answered, less than helpfully.

In a pit almost a kilometre wide and a hundred metres deep, crawling with men and machinery? Without getting caught?

Yeah, that's about it.

Great.

She risked a look over the top of the pile of rocks, then ducked down, swearing.

A yellow pickup truck was heading her way.

REX MAJOR HAD JUST ENDURED a tour of the water treatment facilities and was trudging dutifully back down a long, dull corridor toward the entry hall when shouts and the sound of slamming doors broke out somewhere ahead of them.

"What's going on?" he asked Ursu, grateful for anything to interrupt the extremely detailed guided tour his host seemed determined to inflict on him. Even worse, for the sake of appearances—and because it just might help him find the shard of Excalibur—he had to pretend to find it all interesting.

Ursu frowned. "I don't know." He hurried ahead.

Just outside the grandly named Visitor Orientation Centre—a smallish room containing a table, some chairs, a TV, a lot of brochures and DVDs—a security guard the size of a small building held a scrawny red-haired teenage boy with one ham-sized hand while yelling into a walkie-talkie with the other. "I don't know how she did it, but she's gone! Vanished from a windowless washroom! Search the camp! And get that helicopter back! Over!"

The listening boy had a wide, cocky grin on his homely freckled face, but that grin vanished when he saw Ursu and Major.

Major had never seen the kid before, but he had a bad feeling he knew who "she" was. *Vanished from a windowless washroom?*

"The Lady of the Lake!" he growled. Ursu gave him a puzzled glance, but he no longer cared about appearances. He strode forward and grabbed the boy's free arm. "How did you get here?"

The security guard put down the still squawking walkie-talkie. "You know him?"

"Never saw him before in my life. But I know why he's here." Major shook the boy's arm. The kid winced. "Well?"

"Like I told Drea here, we were camping with our parents—"

"Don't give me that bull," the guard snapped. "The helicopter pilot has reported back. No one is camped west of here within fifty klicks."

The boy's eyes widened. "Then what happened to our parents? You'd better start a search—"

"Enough!" roared Major. He tightened his grip on the

boy's arm. Reaching inside for the pitiful trickle of power that still flowed to him from Faerie, he spoke with the Voice of Command that had once set whole armies marching to his will. "Tell me."

The boy's grin went out like a light. "The Lady of the Lake spoke to us," he said in a voice turned dull and strained. "She gave Ariane her power. She warned us that you had awakened and were trying to find the shards of Excalibur. We came here through rivers and lakes to stop you."

"Where is the girl now?" Major ignored the bewildered stares of the security guards and Ursu.

"I don't know. She must have gone down the drain. She's probably picking up the shard of Excalibur right now." The flicker of defiance in the boy's voice astonished Major: the Voice of Command should have extinguished it.

Major released the boy and turned to the others. *"Forget what this boy and I have just said!"* he Commanded them all. "I'd like to see your security headquarters, please," he then said to Ursu in his usual business tone.

Ursu opened his mouth as though intending to ask a question, then blinked, bewildered, as if he'd forgotten what he'd been about to say. "Um . . . of course. This way."

"She'll find it first!" the boy called after Major, and that astonished him all over again: the boy had not responded to his final Command.

"Shut up," the guard said. "You and I will wait in here." He shoved the boy into the Visitor Orientation Centre.

Who is that boy? Major knew he would have to find out— but not now. The girl could be anywhere. *She may already have the shard . . .*

No. I would feel it. There's still time.

Ursu led him to the end of the long corridor they'd been following earlier, then into the utilidor he had pointed out from the airplane. The prefabricated, lightly insulated tunnel must have been ice-cold in the winter, but at least it blocked the wind. Security cameras watched it at ten-metre intervals. It ended in a locked door that Ursu opened with a swipe of a keycard. On the other side of the door another corridor ran left and right—west and east, if Major could still trust his sense of direction. A few metres away, both corridors turned north again. Ursu led Major to the right. When they turned north, he saw two more doors: one on the left, about ten metres down, the other farther down on the right, near the end of the corridor.

Ursu took him to the door on the left. Instead of using his keycard, he looked up at a camera above the door. "Ursu here with Rex Major. Mr. Major would like to inspect our security."

"Come on in, Mr. Ursu, Mr. Major," an intercom-distorted woman's voice said. The door hummed and clicked, then swung outward. Ursu stepped aside and gestured for Major to enter first, then followed him in. The door closed behind them.

Inside, another short corridor led to another door. They went through it (it, too, closed behind them automatically) into a large square room lined with TV monitors, computer screens, communications equipment and, somewhat incongruously, a bright red Coke machine and a vending machine full of chips and candy bars. Empty paper coffee cups and old magazines littered a glass-topped coffee table in front of a greasy looking black leather couch. A short, solid woman with close-cropped red hair slouched in a swivel chair in front of a control panel. "Hello, Verone," Ursu said. "This is Rex Major."

Verone barely glanced at him before turning back to her console. "Pleased to meet you."

"Can you see every part of the compound from here?" Major asked Ursu.

"Pretty much," Ursu said. "There are a few blind spots, but they're not near anything crucial and the approaches to them are well-covered. There are also motion sensors, infrared sensors and cameras for nighttime use. We can track anything that moves."

"And there's no sign of the girl?"

Ursu glanced at the woman. "Verone?"

"She's not in the compound," Verone said. "And the helicopter pilot hasn't spotted her, either."

"Have you checked the pit?" Major asked.

Verone gave him a scornful look. "There's no way she could get to the pit without us seeing her . . . sir."

Major quelled a surge of anger. *In the old days, such insolence would not have gone unpunished!* "Do you have cameras in the pit?" He kept his annoyance out of his voice.

"Yes, but—"

"*Show me*," Major Commanded.

Verone's mouth fell open. She blinked hard a couple of times, then spun in her chair and punched a few buttons. Four screens flickered and switched to images of the huge open pit to the east. Major leaned in close. In the far distance of one camera shot, a pickup truck rolled to a stop beside a pile of rock. Two men got out.

As they did so, a third figure leaped up from behind the rock pile and ran for the truck. "Zoom in!"

Verone grabbed the joystick poking up from the centre of her console and shoved it forward. The pickup truck seemed to leap toward the camera, filling the screen just in time for Major to see a teenage girl scramble into the driver's seat and slam the door shut.

"There she is!" he cried. "Tell your men to stop her!"

Verone jabbed a button and shouted into a microphone: "All security personnel! Intruder in the pit—she's just grabbed Pickup 27. Stop her!" Then she turned to Major. "There aren't any security people in the pit, sir. It will be a few minutes before anyone can get there." Her tone was properly respectful, this time—a pleasant side effect of the Voice of Command.

"How can I get there?"

"I don't think that's a good idea," Ursu protested.

"Tell me!" Major Commanded Verone, and winced as an icepick of pain stabbed him above his left eye. He was using the Voice too much, but this was an emergency.

"You can use my vehicle. It's just outside." Verone handed him the keys. "The exit is at the end of the corridor."

Major grabbed the keys and was out the door before Ursu could splutter another objection.

12

INTRUDER IN THE PIT

ARIANE DIDN'T KNOW she was going to steal the pickup until she did it. But as she knelt in the mud behind the rock pile, hoping against hope the men in the approaching truck wouldn't find her, the song of the shard sharpened yet again, calling out to her.

It knows I'm near!

She closed her eyes and concentrated, trying to home in on that song with her mind the way she would home in on a sound in the ordinary world . . . and then, as though yet another unsuspected aspect of the Lady's power had suddenly sprung to life inside her, she had it. In her own backyard, listening with her eyes closed, she could get some sense of which of the trees a bird was chirping from. This was something like that, but far more accurate, as if she could tell not only which tree the bird was in, but on which twig it perched. She knew, without a doubt, that the shard was . . . *there*, not quite in the centre of the pit, and not on the surface, but not too deeply buried, either.

Then the pickup pulled up on the opposite side of the pile, and the two men got out of it and walked toward the pond in which she'd materialized, leaving the truck running. Almost without thinking, she leaped up and ran. The men shouted as she darted past, but they were slow, way too slow, and before they had closed half the distance back to the truck she was in the driver's seat. Grateful for the Driver's Ed she'd had in her last semester at her previous school, she jammed the transmission into drive and shoved her foot down hard. In the rearview mirror she saw the men duck as the spinning tires hurled gravel in their faces, then she fish-tailed the truck around and headed for the centre of the pit . . . and the shard of Excalibur.

"All security personnel!" the radio squawked. "Intruder in the pit—she's just grabbed Pickup 27. Stop her!"

She ignored the voice. All that mattered was the shard, calling her, pulling her to it. Its song filled her mind, flooding out all fear. In minutes it would be hers. She floored the accelerator. There were pits and piles of rock to manoeuvre around, and she attacked the winding path like a rally driver, spewing gravel and dusty snow at every turn. A bulldozer backed into her path, and she spun the wheel savagely to the left, then to the right, catching a glimpse of the driver's wide eyes as the pickup's right-side mirror snapped off against the bulldozer's rear end. She skidded and roared on.

In the centre of the pit, the giant mining shovel continued to dig and roar, like some prehistoric monster.

She was heading straight for it.

Drezner and Wally's staring contest in the Visitor Orientation Centre was interrupted by the crackle of Drezner's walkie-talkie. "All security personnel! Intruder in the pit —she's just grabbed Pickup 27. Stop her!"

Drezner swore and jumped to his feet. He grabbed Wally's arm and hustled him back outside to the pickup truck they'd arrived in, shoving him through the passenger door so hard he sprawled across the seat. "Hey, not so rough!" Wally protested. Drezner slammed the door on him, then dashed around the front of the pickup. As Wally pulled himself upright, Drezner threw open the door on the driver's side and clambered in.

"She escaped from me," Drezner snarled, twisting the ignition key as though he'd like to break it off. "If anyone's going to get her back, it's going to be me."

Wally grinned. "Good luck. She's pretty slippery." Drezner shot him a fierce glare, then slammed the pickup into drive and stomped down hard on the gas pedal.

"She's heading for the centre of the pit," said the radio. Then, "She's going to get herself killed if she doesn't watch out!"

Ariane wasn't unaware of the gigantic digging machine looming over her, but it seemed unreal, unimportant. What was real, what mattered, was the shard singing in her head, calling to her, calling to the blood and the power of the Lady of the Lake, its creator and guardian. And then that song became an overwhelming shout that flooded her senses so thoroughly it almost blotted out the world around her. She slammed on the brakes as the inside of the truck faded from her vision and the roaring of the giant shovel subsided to a faint growl.

The only thing that remained clear and sharp in her vision was the last great gash in the gravel made by the shovel. The giant bucket's edge had caught and lifted the end of an enormous slab of rock within that gash, and water glittered in the dark space underneath.

And in that water . . .

She threw open the door of the pickup and stepped inside a deepening shadow that suddenly made it hard to see beneath the slab. Annoyed, she looked up to see what was blocking the light—and fear burst through the song of the sword, trapping her breath inside her chest.

The huge steel bucket was dropping toward her for another bite of gravel, far too fast for her to leap out of the way.

What happened next was out of her conscious control, pure survival instinct, the ancient imperative to draw on every resource the body could command when death threatened. Driven by adrenalin and terror, the power of the Lady reached out for the nearest water—and found the pool beneath the huge rock slab that sheltered the first shard of Excalibur.

The water exploded out of its hiding place, lifting the slab as easily as a gust of wind would lift a leaf. Thick mud splattered the ground around Ariane, but not a drop touched her. The slab smashed into the descending bucket with an earsplitting crash, driving it up and backward, shifting the whole massive shovel over the lip of the shallow slope to its right. Cables snapped, whining like angry bees as they wrapped themselves around the shovel's structure. The rock slab crashed to the ground just metres from Ariane, shaking the earth. The shovel, unbalanced, began to tip. The operator scrambled out and jumped clear just as it fell ponderously onto its side down the slope, where it lay, twisted and useless.

Ariane had already forgotten about it. Now that she had removed the slab, Excalibur's song slammed into her mind with as much force as the slab had slammed into the shovel. Her knees buckled. She dropped to all fours, then scrambled to the edge of the gaping hole the shovel had just opened, drawn like a moth to a candle flame.

Every drop of water had exploded out of the hole and left it bone-dry. She slid down the slope on her rear, landing on her feet in a cloud of dust.

In the middle of the hole, sunlight gleamed off the black, glassy surface of an obsidian box the size of a jewellery case. Ariane knelt beside it, wondering how to open it—but the moment she touched it, it clicked and the lid lifted.

Nestled inside a bed of fibrous dust that might once have been cloth was a sharply pointed piece of age-pitted and darkened steel, about twenty centimetres long and a bit under four centimetres wide, honed on two sides, and broken off at the top.

Ariane reached for it. The instant she touched the shard, its already nearly overwhelming song crescendoed to such a fortissimo of joy and delight that, dazed, she fell ungracefully —and painfully—onto her bottom.

But as quickly as the song had climaxed, it quieted, as if the shard were relieved to have returned to the hands of the Lady of the Lake.

Or, at least, a reasonable facsimile thereof.

The cessation of the shard's song brought the reality of her situation crashing down on Ariane. She had the shard, but Security had Wally, Rex Major had probably realized by now what she was up to, and she had just destroyed a very large and very valuable piece of equipment.

Just how much do giant mining shovels cost, anyway?

She had to somehow elude Major, find Wally, and get both of them back to Regina. After that . . .

After that, she didn't have a clue.

But first things first.

She clambered up the hole's dusty slope to the floor of the pit. There she pulled herself to her feet, brushed herself off, and finally looked up, intending to get back into her pickup—

—only to see *three* pickups blocking her way, and, standing between her and all of them, Rex Major, his left arm wrapped around Wally's chest, his right hand pressing a pistol to Wally's head.

REX MAJOR HAD SEEN the extraordinary eruption of water, mud and rock smash into the giant shovel, and despite himself, had been impressed. At the peak of his powers, he might have been able to manage such a feat, but not anymore.

Once he had Excalibur whole and in his possession, of course, all that would change—and the first shard of Excalibur had to be right at the girl's feet. Why else would she have stopped where she had, beneath the giant shovel's bucket?

He roared along one of the winding roads leading to the pit's centre. A glance at the rearview mirror showed him the other pickup; it was close enough that he could tell who was in it—the massive security guard, Drezner, and the girl's young companion, the boy who was so resistant to his Voice of Command.

When he looked ahead, he saw the girl had moved into the pit dug by the shovel. She might be putting her hands on the shard at that very moment.

He glanced at the rearview mirror again, and bared his teeth in a feral smile.

She won't have it for long!

THE DESTRUCTION of the shovel made Drezner swear and Wally's jaw drop. Even after everything he had seen Ariane do, he had never imagined she had *that* kind of power. It frightened him a little—heck, more than a little. *I've gotta warn Flish to lay off her, or I may just find myself short a sister!*

"Damn thing must have hit an Artesian well or something," Drezner muttered. "I hope your *sister* is still alive."

"She's alive." Wally had glimpsed her momentarily, before she dropped out of sight into the hole dug by the shovel. *But she may not stay that way for much longer,* he thought, his eyes shifting to Major's pickup ahead of them.

The two trucks raced across the bottom of the mine pit

and braked to a halt within a few metres of each other, next to the mud-covered pickup Ariane had been driving.

As Drezner leaned forward to lift the microphone from the truck's two-way radio, Major burst out of his vehicle and ran toward them. "Drez!" Wally warned.

Drezner, his back to Major, hushed Wally with an impatient chop of his hand and spoke into the mike. "Security Five here. She's in the pit, down in the hole the shovel just dug. Looks like the shovel is a complete write-off. I'll go down there and—"

But just what he'd go down there and do, Wally never heard, for at that moment Major reached the pickup, jerked open the driver's-side door, and snapped one word at Drezner: "*Sleep.*"

Drezner closed his eyes mid-word and slumped in his seat.

"Security Five?" the radio squawked. "Security Five, come in! Drez, what's going on? All our cameras in the pit just went out!"

Major reached inside the cab and pulled Drezner's pistol from its holster, then looked at Wally. His gaze, as blue and cold as a January sky, chilled Wally, who turned and tried to grab the door handle. But Major dashed around the front of the truck and, just as Wally started to push the door, the sorcerer grabbed it and jerked it wide open. Wally tumbled out onto the gravelly ground in a bruised and undignified heap.

Major hauled him to his feet—*Shouldn't a centuries-old man be at least a little bit frail?* Wally thought resentfully—as the wizard twisted his arm behind his back. "You're too late," Wally gasped. "She already has the shard by now."

"She may have it, but she won't keep it." Major began frog-marching him toward the edge of the hole into which Ariane had disappeared. "I've been waiting for this moment for fifteen hundred years. With Excalibur, I can return to my own world and free it from millennia of tyranny. I'm not going to let you, her, or anyone else on Earth stand in my way."

As if on cue, Ariane's head reappeared above the lip of the hole. Merlin pulled Wally into a bear hug with his left arm while his right hand pressed the muzzle of the pistol against the boy's cheek. The cold, hard metal dug into the skin, the pressure so hard it made the bone beneath ache.

Ariane climbed out of the hole, dusted herself off, straightened, saw them—and froze.

Rex Major's face had taken on a harsh, angular appearance, as though the ancient skull beneath his skin had somehow come to the fore. The ruby stud in his right earlobe looked less like the affectation of a modern businessman and more like the barbarous display of an ancient warrior. No one who knew him from his corporate publicity photos would have recognized him. His colleagues and employees would have crossed the street to avoid him.

Unfortunately, Ariane didn't have that option.

"*Give the shard to me,*" Major said in a voice like broken glass. "*Or the boy dies.*"

The Lady's power registered the Voice of Command—and casually parried its feeble thrust. But the power could not protect Wally. Ariane could see how the gun's pressure against Wally's cheek had driven the blood from his skin so that, once again, his freckles stood out like a leopard's spots. She knew that Major would not hesitate to pull the trigger to get what he wanted.

"This whole pit must be on camera," she said. "And there are workers down here. They'll see you threatening Wally. You can't—"

"I have more power than you think," Major said. "The cameras are not working. The witnesses can see nothing but haze and dust. No one will rescue you."

Ariane reached inside herself for her own power, the power that moments ago had been able to hurl tonnes of rock into the air . . . and found nothing.

She didn't have enough energy left to move a raindrop.

If the Lady were to be believed, it would be a disaster for the world if Rex Major were to re-forge Excalibur. She'd told Wally herself in the Human Bean that Merlin would be the worst tyrant in all of history.

But he was holding a gun to her best friend's—her only friend's—head.

It's only one shard.

There were other shards. There would be other opportunities to stop Merlin.

But the shard is mine. The part of her that was the Lady made her fingers tighten around it. *I will not give it up. I will not. I will not—*

Major shoved the pistol harder against Wally's cheek, so hard the boy cried out in pain.

The part of Ariane that was not the Lady made the only possible choice.

There were other shards. But she had no other friends.

"Take it," she said, and held out the shard.

"Ariane—" Wally started, then winced and subsided as Major jabbed him again with the barrel of the pistol.

"Drop it," Major said, no longer trying to Command her.

"Let him go first," Ariane said.

Major smiled. It wasn't a pleasant smile. "I can still kill him," he said. "And *then* take the shard. *Drop it.*"

Ariane held out the shard. She willed her fingers to unclench, to let if fall. For a moment they refused to obey her. Then, convulsively, they snapped open. The shard fell to the ground. She gasped as its song turned discordant, filled with anger that she had let it go.

"Step away from it," Major said.

Ariane backed away toward the pit.

Still holding Wally, Major shuffled forward. When he stood over the shard, he pulled the pistol away from Wally's face and shoved the boy so hard he fell and rolled twice. Ariane hurried to him. By the time she had helped him to his feet, Major was holding the shard in his left hand. He barely glanced at it before he shoved it into his pocket. His right hand still held the pistol, now pointed at both of them. Wally stood panting beside her, one hand rubbing his bruised cheek.

Ariane reached desperately for the Lady's power. All she could call from the mud and snow around her was a fine mist that rose no more than an inch, then subsided.

Major laughed. "Out of steam, are you? Magic takes its toll, girl. Well, save your strength. Your magic can't harm me anyway: that much of my old power remains. Go home and forget you ever saw the Lady, and I promise, I will leave you alone. But get in my way again—well, I have many servants, both human and . . . not. You can't escape them all."

"You can't hurt me, or you already would have!" Ariane flung at him, hoping it was the truth.

"It's true I can't *kill* you—not yet," Major said. "Now that you have the Lady's power, to kill you would be to destroy that power, and the power of Excalibur with it. But I *can* hurt you. Or lock you away where no one will ever find you. Or both." Major showed his teeth in a savage grin. "And even the dubious protection from death you enjoy doesn't extend to those around you—as your boyfriend just discovered. As your aunt can be taught."

Ariane felt the blood drain from her face.

"If you are fortunate—and smart—we will not meet again." Without turning his back on Ariane, Major edged toward to the pickup in which Wally had arrived. At the open door, he spun around and replaced the pistol in the security chief's holster, then Commanded Drezner: *"Wake!"*

The big guard suddenly sat upright, and Major shouted, "There she is!"

As though he had never been asleep, Drezner leaped out of the truck and drew his gun. "All right, you," he growled. "You're coming with me." He reached into the pickup again and picked up the microphone. "Security Five here," he said without taking his eyes off Ariane. "I've got her." He frowned, glanced at the pickup's passenger seat, then looked over at Wally, still sitting on the ground where Rex had thrown him. The frown gave way to a confused look. "Uh, both of them, I mean."

Behind Drezner, Rex Major bowed once to Ariane, then got into his own pickup and drove away.

13

SINKS, POOLS, AND TOILETS

The sorely puzzled Drezner cuffed Ariane and Wally. He saw the spreading bruise on the boy's cheek and pointed. "How'd *that* happen?" But neither Wally nor Ariane answered him.

What's the point? Ariane thought. No one but them had seen what Major had done, and Drezner apparently had no idea he'd even been asleep. He'd never believe a wild story of a successful businessman like Rex Major threatening a teenage boy with a stolen gun. Ariane could already see him brushing away his curiosity like an annoying insect.

The radio crackled, and Ariane heard Major's voice over the open radio channel. "Security? Rex Major here."

"Mr. Major!" Ursu's voice crackled back at once. "Where are you?"

"Just driving out of the pit. It looks like your people have your little problem under control." *A little problem,* Ariane thought bitterly. *That's all I was.*

"This is highly unusual, Mr. Major. I assure you, we rarely have—"

"No need to apologize, Mr. Ursu. I was very impressed by the professionalism of your security staff. Very impressed. And, I might add, impressed by everything else I've seen today."

"I'm pleased to hear it, Mr. Major." Ursu sounded relieved. "I'd still like to show you the crushing facility, if you've—"

"That won't be necessary—or possible. I'm afraid I must ask to be flown back to Yellowknife immediately."

"So soon? But there's so much—"

"I've seen enough, Mr. Ursu. I'll be directing my financial people to make a sizeable investment in your company. Once I'm back in Yellowknife, we can finalize matters."

A pause. "Really? I mean, that's wonderful but—"

"Have the pilot meet me at the airfield immediately. I trust that won't be a problem."

"No, sir." Another pause, filled with the indistinct murmur of voices in the background, then Ursu said, "He's on his way."

"Thank you, Mr. Ursu. You've been most helpful."

The radio crackled and went silent.

That's it, then, Ariane thought. *He'll be gone before we're even out of the pit.* She leaned her head back against the tire and closed her eyes, letting her exhaustion take her.

"Taking a nap?" Drezner's voice snapped her back to wakefulness. "Get up." He pushed her and Wally through the pickup's open passenger door and rounded the front of the truck to climb into the driver's seat. As he started the engine, he glanced at Ariane. "I don't know how you got away last time, young lady, but don't think you can manage it again. I'm not letting you out of my sight."

Ariane said nothing. She could feel her power seeping back . . . but slowly, so slowly. Food or sleep might bring it back faster, but there seemed little chance of either.

She'd just have to wait.

They drove out of the pit, passing half a dozen trucks headed the other way, probably full of maintenance workers and mine officials going to have a look at the crippled shovel. Ariane had no doubt she'd cost the company hundreds of thousands of dollars. *And I didn't even manage to hang on to the shard. I actually made it easier for Merlin to get it! Lady of the Lake? What a joke!*

She leaned her head against the cool glass of the window and stared at the ground rolling past, wishing she had never heard the singing of the water in Wascana Lake.

WALLY GLANCED AT ARIANE. It didn't take a mind reader to see she was upset. He couldn't blame her. He felt more than a little low himself. *Some Companion of the Order of the Lady. Kidnapped by the villain. Used to blackmail the heroine. I should have stayed home.*

He touched his bruised cheek and winced. He'd been bullied his entire life, thanks to being both small and smart, but no one had ever threatened to kill him before—not someone who really meant it anyway (Flish didn't count). It proved Major's—Merlin's—ruthlessness, of course, proved he couldn't be allowed to get Excalibur . . . but there was something Major had said, about needing the sword to free his own world from tyranny, and waiting fifteen centuries for this moment, that had struck a chord in Wally. He could almost sympathize with him . . . probably *would* have sympathized with him, if he had been a character in a book. Locked away without magic for centuries, freed at last but almost powerless, fighting to free his world? When you thought about it that way, Rex Major was a character straight out of a fantasy epic.

Wally snorted. *He's Merlin. Of* course *he's a character straight out of a fantasy epic!*

They rolled out over the lip of the pit, and Wally saw a Twin Otter lifting into the sky from the airfield beyond the lake. "Major, headed back to Yellowknife," Drezner commented. "And after he finishes up his business, he'll be heading to Toronto." He leaned forward to see the plane better. "Lucky dog. I'm stuck here six more weeks before I get any leave."

Finishes up his business? An idea suddenly blossomed in Wally's head. What had Major said? *"Once I'm back in Yellowknife, we can finalize matters."*

He's not heading straight back to Toronto, he thought. *He could be in Yellowknife for hours. There's still time!* Wally glanced at Ariane. *We have to talk . . .*

But Ariane didn't seem to have noticed the exchange. Her head remained pressed against the glass, and her eyes stayed closed. Wally could only imagine her exhaustion. How much energy would it take to lift a slab of rock that size that high and that fast?

He spent the rest of the short ride trying to calculate it, but hadn't managed to figure it out before they rolled to a stop in front of the main building. Drezner ushered them inside. "The Mounties are on their way. They'll be here in a couple of hours. Then we'll get to the bottom of this. For now, you can cool your heels." He knocked on the glass of the reception booth. The guard inside, who had switched from *Sports Illustrated* to a five-year-old *National Geographic*, looked up and frowned. "What is it, Drez?"

"Is 104 still empty, Ben?"

Ben heaved an exaggerated sigh, put down his magazine, and tapped the computer keyboard to his right. He peered at the screen. "Until the crew refresh next Saturday."

"Let me have the key."

Ben sighed again, hauled his rather large bulk out of the chair, and disappeared from sight. He returned with a keycard and slid it through the small square opening at the bottom of the glass window that separated him from the world. "Is that all?" His tone implied that it had better be.

"Yeah. Thanks." Drezner slipped the keycard into his shirt pocket, then took Wally's arm with one hand and Ariane's with the other. "I'm going to lock you in one of the apartments until the Mounties get here. But don't think you can use the time to get your stories straight because I'm going to be with you every second."

To Wally's surprise, Ariane spoke for the first time since Drezner had loaded them into the pickup. "What if I have to go to the bathroom? Are you going to follow me in?"

"Maybe I should, since you got out of one locked bathroom already," Drezner growled, but then he unclipped the walkie-talkie from his belt and said into it, "Security One, this is Security Five, over."

"Security One here. You got those kids locked up yet, Drez? Over."

"Just about. I'm going to put them in 104. But I need a female guard too, to watch the girl in case she . . . you know. Can you send Jenny down? Over."

"Roger that, Drez. I'll have her there in two minutes. Over."

"Thanks. Over and out."

Drezner clipped the walkie-talkie back onto his belt. "Satisfied?"

Great, Wally thought. *Her best chance to get away, and she blew it.*

Not that it would help *him* if she pulled a disappearing-from-the-bathroom act again.

Drezner led them down the corridor to the main hallway, and across it through fire doors into what looked for all the world like a hotel—not a fancy Banff Springs kind of hotel, maybe, but at least a Travelodge in Moose Jaw. The door Drezner opened with the keycard, though, led not into a hotel room but into a small—very small—apartment, with its own kitchenette, a separate bedroom and a bathroom located just inside the front door. The main living room featured a couch, a desk, bookshelves, a TV (complete with a video game console) and a couple of big armchairs covered in leather dyed an unfortunate shade of purple.

Wally barely had time to take all that in before someone said "knock, knock" behind them. He turned to see another security guard, a skinny blonde with pouty lips, an angular face and way too much eye shadow.

"Hi, Jenny," Drezner said. "Will you watch the door?"

She nodded.

Drezner settled into one of the chairs. "Make yourselves at home," he told Wally and Ariane.

Jenny dragged one of the two chairs away from the tiny dining table, placed it in front of the door, and then sat down on it and leaned back, legs stretched out, arms folded, face impassive.

Wally looked at Ariane, then at the kitchenette sink. She followed his glance, but turned away from the kitchenette and sat down on the couch. Not knowing what else to do, Wally sat next to her. "I guess we wait, then?"

"I guess you do," Drezner replied, though Wally had aimed the question at Ariane. Her only response was to lean back and close her eyes.

Drezner picked up the remote control from the arm of his chair and turned on the TV. Two men were scrubbing little brooms against a sheet of ice, trying to stay ahead of a round chunk of granite with a blue handle on top of it. "You like curling?"

Wally groaned. "No!"

The sliding rock slammed into a stationary one with a sound like a thunderclap. The crowd roared. Drezner shrugged. "Too bad."

For the next hour and a half, Wally watched sliding rocks and men with brooms while Ariane napped, or so it seemed. Nobody said anything. After forty-five minutes, Drezner changed places with Jenny. She sat just as silently as he had, staring at the TV.

Finally, ninety minutes later, Ariane opened her eyes and stood up.

ARIANE KNEW VERY WELL what Wally had meant by his pointed look at the sink. She hadn't missed the significance of Rex Major stopping in Yellowknife before returning to Toronto either. In Toronto, he would have the shard locked up, and unless his safe had running water, they'd never be able to get their hands on it. But in Yellowknife . . .

If only she wasn't so tired!

Drezner had said the Mounties would arrive in "a couple of hours." So, while Wally suffered through curling, she dozed, trying not to use any more energy than she had to.

She needed even more time to fully recover . . . but they were running out of it.

She stood up. Wally's eyes snapped to her. So did Drezner's. So did Jenny's. She tried to keep her voice casual. "Anything to eat in the kitchen?"

"I doubt it," Drezner said. "Place should have been emptied out when the guy living here went south."

"Mind if I take a look? I'm starving."

Drezner shrugged. "Go wild."

She glanced at Wally. "Want to help?"

Wally grinned. "Sure!"

She winced. *Don't sound so eager!* But Drezner's gaze had already shifted back to the TV.

Ariane made a show of searching the cabinets while Wally looked in the refrigerator. Except for a stack of plastic cups, an empty two-litre Coke bottle and a box of sugar cubes (Ariane ate six—calories were calories), the shelves were empty.

Wally closed the refrigerator. "Nothing in there but a bad smell."

Ariane took a couple of cups from the stack and handed

one to Wally. "Guess we'll have to settle for a drink of water."

Wally grinned again. "Good. I'm thirsty."

Ariane turned on the tap.

"They have really good water up here," Wally said. "At least, they do in Yellowknife."

She almost laughed. "So I've heard."

"What are you two up to in there?" Drezner stood up from his chair and took a couple of steps toward them. "You're wasting water."

Ariane hardly heard him. The water had begun to call to her the moment she turned on the tap, but what she needed to hear was the song of the sword . . . and there it was, a faint echo of what she had heard in the pit, but much stronger than it had been in Regina. West . . . and south.

Yellowknife. It had to be.

"Just running it to get it cold," Wally said.

Ariane touched the stream of water, and felt the power surge within her—not as strong as it had been at its peak, but strong enough. She grabbed Wally's hand. Some perverse impulse made her call, "'Bye, Drez. 'Bye, Jenny. Wish I could say it's been fun—but it hasn't."

She delayed long enough to see Jenny leap up from the couch and Drezner lunge toward them—and then she let the flow take them. She heard the beginning of twin shouts before everything vanished.

They rushed through the pipes to the sewage treatment plant, through the outflow pipe into the depths of a lake, through rivers, muskeg and underground aquifers. She followed the song of the sword, feeling the shard grow closer and closer—until she knew they were as close as they could get.

They emerged in warm water that stung her eyes. She straightened her legs, and her feet touched concrete instead of mud.

She found herself standing beside Wally in a swimming pool. A little girl, maybe four years old, stared wide-eyed at them from the coils of a floating green plastic donut with the head of a dragon. "You shouldn't go swimming with your clothes on," she said.

Ariane smiled at her. "You're right!" She looked around. Three older children, two girls and a boy, and a couple of very startled-looking adults stared back from the other end of the pool, which was inside a three-story greenhouse-like structure attached to a larger building. Waterslides towered at one end. Balconies with sliding glass doors overlooked the pool on the building side, which they were facing. Behind them, outside the moisture-fogged glass, sunlight glared off deep snow. Inside, the temperature was tropical.

It's a hotel, Ariane thought. *Major must be staying here.*

"Hey! You kids get out of there!" A man in a blue janitor's uniform appeared from behind the waterslides.

"Yes, sir!" Ariane called. She and Wally climbed from the pool using the nearest ladder. They stood dripping on the tiled side of the pool while the janitor gave them a long lecture about fouling the pool and the dangers of drowning and where were their parents anyway? He ended by banning them from the pool for the rest of their stay and told them to get out before he reported them to the management.

Trying to look sheepish, they slipped past the giggling kids, lined up on the edge of the pool like spectators at a water polo match. A short carpeted corridor, with doors leading to the men's and women's change areas, connected the pool area to the lobby. By the time they reached the end of it, they were dry but the walls were dripping. *Serves the old guy right*, Ariane thought, then felt a little guilty—the janitor hadn't really done anything they didn't deserve, from his point of view—but there really was nowhere else to send the water.

They entered the lobby. Two armchairs upholstered in green plaid stood on either side of an artificial fireplace, and Ariane led Wally to them. "OK," she said in a low voice once they were both seated. "That was the easy part. Now we have to figure out how to get into Major's room and find the shard."

"Wait until he's taking a bath and materialize in his bathtub?" Wally suggested.

"Uh . . . no." But the mental image of the two of them emerging in a bathtub while a naked Major stared at them, shocked, made her grin a little—and then a lot when she thought of all the water their arrival would spill across the bathtub floor. "Got it! What we need is a diversion . . . and a way to get into Major's room."

"What if he's in it?"

"Then we'll wait until he isn't," Ariane said.

"First we need to figure out which room it is," Wally pointed out.

"Shouldn't be hard. In fact, let's do it right now." She hopped out of the chair and cocked her head, listening to the song of Excalibur, coming from . . . "Follow me."

A hallway ran the length of the building. They entered a stairwell at one end and climbed up to the first landing, where Ariane hesitated, listening. "At least one more floor . . ." Up another flight. "This one." Into the hallway. "Other wing." Past the elevators. The shard's song was so loud now she could hardly believe Wally couldn't hear it. She placed her hands on the wall, and began walking slowly along the corridor, running her fingers over the paint. Stronger . . . stronger . . . and then, suddenly, weaker. She backed up. "Here!"

Wally checked the room number: 303. "OK, so now how do we make sure he's not in there with it?" he whispered.

Ariane led him back down to the lobby, and picked up the handset of a white courtesy phone on the desk. She dialled Major's room number, listened for a moment, then hung up. "No answer. He's not in there."

"And here I thought you'd use magic," Wally said. They left the lobby, and this time took the elevator to the third floor. As the door opened and they stepped into the hallway, he said, "So, what's your diversion?"

"Watch." Once again standing outside Room 303, Ariane pressed her forehead against the wall, feeling for water. "Got it," she whispered, and *tugged*.

A rumbling in the wall, a gurgling, a loud clanking sound —and Ariane stepped back, smiling.

"Now what?" Wally said.

"Now we run downstairs and tell them the toilet in our room overflowed."

"The toilet in *our* . . . oh!" He laughed. "Sweet!"

They raced back down the stairs and down the hall, but Ariane stopped Wally before they reached the lobby. "Allow me," she said. She sauntered into the lobby and banged on the bell on the desk. A clerk emerged.

"Yes, miss?"

"There's something, like, wrong with the toilet in our uncle's room?" Ariane said, trying to sound both bored and annoyed and making sure to add a little uptick at the end of each sentence to make everything sound like a question. "There's, like, water running all over the floor? And, like, into the corridor and everything? It's really gross?"

The desk clerk looked stricken. "I'm so sorry, miss! We'll have that looked after right away." He grabbed the phone. "Maintenance, we've got a broken toilet in Room—" he looked at Ariane and Wally.

"303," Wally supplied with a helpful smile.

"303. Hurry, please."

"Our uncle is going to be so bummed," Ariane said. She heaved an exaggerated sigh, and then sauntered back out of the lobby. The moment they were out of sight of the concierge, she grabbed Wally's arm and ran to the elevator.

"Uncle?" Wally said.

"He's going to look up who's in Room 303," she said. "He may know who Rex Major is, but there's no way he can be sure we're not Major's niece and nephew."

"Smart," Wally said.

They exited the elevator on the third floor and strode down the hall to where, sure enough, a dark stain was spreading across the blue-green carpet beneath the door to Room 303.

The janitor who showed up a moment later, a little out of breath, was the same man who had ordered them out of the pool. His eyes widened. "You two! What did you do this time?"

"Nothing," Wally said, which was true—for him. "The water just suddenly came over the top of the toilet."

The janitor grunted. "Likely story." He used his passkey to open the room. While he walked into the bathroom, Ariane and Wally moved over the soaking carpet into the main room.

The room looked unused, except for a single soft-sided suitcase that lay on a stand below the curtained window, and a closed laptop computer on the desk.

The shard sang to Ariane from the suitcase. She wondered why Major had left it unattended . . . and when he would be back. They might not have much time. She hurried to the suitcase and tried to open it . . .

. . . and only then saw the bright orange miniature padlocks that held each zipper closed.

"It's locked," Ariane whispered to Wally.

He fingered the locks, then glanced back at the bathroom. "I've got an idea," he said. He tiptoed toward the bathroom, and Ariane, wondering what he was up to, followed him.

As they came close to the door, she could see the janitor's boots and hear his muttered cursing. He was kneeling on the floor pulling at something in the toilet tank. His back was to them. All she could see was his rear end . . .

. . . and his tool belt. Wally pointed, and Ariane followed the gesture. Hanging from the belt was a heavy pair of tin snips, the kind plumbers used. "I'll distract him, you grab," he whispered.

"What? Wait—"

But Wally didn't wait. He stepped into the room. "Can I

help?" he said eagerly. He leaned over the toilet tank. "What's that thing do?"

"Don't touch—" The janitor reached into the tank as Wally pulled on something. The toilet flushed, more water poured over the edges of the bowl, the janitor swore, and in all the confusion Ariane jumped forward and pulled the snips from the tool belt. Then she turned and dashed for the suitcase.

"Hey!" The janitor tried to get to his feet, but was understandably hampered by having his hand in a toilet tank and water running over his pants. Wally was faster. He escaped the bathroom on Ariane's heels and slammed the door behind him. Then he grabbed its handle with both hands and held on with all his strength while the janitor yelled furiously on the other side and tried to pull it open. "Hurry!" he panted.

The tin snips made short work of the padlocks. She unzipped the suitcase and flicked it open. "Ariane!" Wally said urgently.

She plunged her hands into the clothes inside the suitcase, feeling through shirts, underwear, slacks . . . and there it was, something hard, inside a pair of socks. She tried to pull it out . . .

And couldn't. She might as well have been trying to lift a building.

Magic. She tugged uselessly at the sock that held the shard while the janitor continued to jerk the door handle and roar expletives. "Ariane!" Wally yelled. "Quick!"

Ariane closed her eyes, tried to reach inside herself as she had in the séance—the "meditation exercise"—with the candle in her bedroom. She couldn't counteract magic with physical strength. She needed her own magical power, the Lady's power. But how . . .?

And then she realized the answer had been right in front of her all along. She quit tugging at the sock and concentrated instead on the shard. Its song was urgent, powerful. As she had in the pit, she felt that the shard *wanted* to be with her, *wanted* to come to her. All she had to do was . . .

. . . call it.

Into Ariane's head spilled a new song, her own song, the language of the sword, the music of the water. It welled up into her throat and she heard herself singing out loud. And just like that, the shard released itself, the point slicing through Major's sock and his spell as easily as a knife through butter.

Ariane stopped singing and opened her eyes. The shard rested in her right hand. Its song rang in her head, the essence of joy. On impulse, she raised it to her lips and kissed its cold metal before slipping it into her pocket.

"Ariane!" Wally shouted as the doorknob slipped out of his hands. The janitor slammed the door open and emerged like an angry bull.

"What the hell are you playing at?" he roared. "You're coming down to the . . ." And then his gaze slid to the open suitcase and the pieces of padlock littering the carpet. "What the . . .?"

Wally backed away from him. Ariane scuttled sideways to join Wally.

"Forget talking to the manager, you're going to be talking to the police," the janitor snapped. He stepped out of the bathroom, his feet making squishing noises in the soaking-wet carpet.

"It's not what it looks like," Ariane said, taking Wally's hand. She pushed down with her right foot, and heard a satisfying squelch.

The janitor stepped forward. "Come on," he said. "Give back whatever you took." He held out his hand . . .

. . . and Ariane let the water in the carpet take them away, into the bathroom, into the overflowing toilet, down into the sewers.

Ariane regretted for a moment that she wouldn't be around to hear the janitor try to explain to his boss exactly what had happened to the two kids who had been giving him trouble all morning . . .

. . . or to see what happened when Rex Major returned.

❧ 14 ❧

A THING OF WAR

DURING THE APPROACH TO YELLOWKNIFE, the minute he had cellphone coverage, Rex Major called the Learjet's pilot and asked him how soon they could depart for Toronto.

"No sooner than six this evening," the pilot said. "I was expecting more downtime, so I've been doing some routine maintenance checks. Sorry, sir."

"No problem," Major said, though the delay grated at him. He glanced at Ursu. "I'll go back to the hotel until then. I have some business to conduct anyway."

Ursu beamed. "I radioed my staff before we left the mine," he said. "They're already preparing a draft agreement. I'll have them send it over to the hotel and we can go over it before you head south."

Major admired the executive's decisiveness. *If Pritchard was more like this one,* he thought, *the girl would have been taken care of in Regina.* He would have his human resources people make an approach to Ursu in a few weeks. Until he re-forged the shard and took power, he would need talented people around him.

So it was in the lounge just off the lobby that the hotel's manager found Rex Major, sitting with Ursu, papers spread on the table before them. White-faced, his hands clasped together so tightly his knuckles had turned white, the hotelier said, "Mr. Major. There's been . . . an incident."

Major stared at him. "An incident? What sort of incident?"

"With your luggage . . ."

Major felt cold. *No! She couldn't have . . .*

"What happened?" he growled.

The manager led him into the offices tucked out of sight behind the front desk and mutely pointed to his suitcase, lying on a table. Next to it were the broken remnants of the locks he had put on it before he left.

Major stepped forward and unzipped the suitcase, telling himself it didn't matter, that the protective spell he had placed on the sock he had wrapped the shard in would still have prevented Ariane from . . .

. . . but he knew even as he reached inside that it had not. Like the locks, the spell had been broken. It had vanished as if it had never been . . . and so had the shard.

"How did this happen?" he snarled, turning on the hapless manager, who shrank back with real fear in his eyes.

"A couple of kids, one said she was your niece . . . somehow they tricked the janitor into . . ." The manager's voice trailed away. "Mr. Major, I can't apologize enough. I haven't contacted the police, I didn't know if you'd want that, but if something was stolen I—"

Much as part of him wanted to strike the grovelling

manager down where he stood, as he certainly would have in Arthur's day, that wasn't an option for Rex Major. "Nothing was stolen," he said, injecting icy calmness into his voice. "I don't keep anything of value in my suitcase. But I trust you will review your security procedures. And rest assured that neither I nor any member of my organization will ever stay in this establishment again."

He turned and strode out of the office while the manager was still trying to fumble for more ways to apologize.

The flight to Toronto was long, and Major spent it brooding.

As soon as he had settled in his seat, he checked his email and discovered a note from Human Resources telling him that their Regina sales manager, Keith Pritchard, had been arrested for breaking and entering. A middle-aged woman, one Phyllis Forsythe, armed only with a baseball bat, had nabbed him the moment he had crawled through her second-floor window. He was also accused of stalking a teenage girl. He had of course been suspended immediately and his assistant sales manager had taken over the local operation. Communications was handling the public relations fallout, but didn't feel it would need a statement from him since the matter was purely local.

Ariane had ignored the first warning through her computer. She had somehow escaped Pritchard's attempt to abduct her on the street. Even the "Lizardoid" hadn't scared her off.

Major shook his head. He had exhausted himself preparing that spell which, installed in the girl's computer via email, had opened a passage to the demon world, allowing one of its denizens to take the form of a monster from a computer game . . . but that attack had depended on Ariane's computer remaining connected to the Internet and thus to his power. The connection had been broken before the demon fully materialized, hurling it back into its own world.

The demon would not have killed her—he'd made sure of that in crafting the spell—but it could have killed the boy, or her aunt. Just the presence of such a thing in her bedroom should have terrified her into giving up . . . but it hadn't. She'd not only found the shard, she'd claimed it before he had—*and* stolen it back from him after he'd extorted it from her. Now he faced the unpleasant fact, one he hoped she didn't realize (as she had the truth about his inability to kill her), that he couldn't take it from her by force. He couldn't have pulled it from her hand in the mine pit even if she had been in his grasp instead of the boy.

The shard *wanted* to be with the Lady of the Lake. And now that it was in her possession again, it would cling to her as it had once clung to Arthur, to whom it had been freely given—and as it would never cling to him, who sought to claim it against its creator's will. *Not until I re-forge it! Then it will be mine.* But to re-forge the sword, he needed *all* the scattered pieces of the sword, and to get the first one back, he would have to once again persuade Ariane to give it up of her own free will, as she had in the pit.

Frightening her hadn't worked. But threatening someone she loved . . . it had worked at the pit. It could work again.

And there was something else he could do. The Lady, he was certain, could no longer manifest herself physically through the tiny sliver of an opening left in the door between Faerie and Earth, not after he had pushed her back out of the world on the day she had contacted Ariane. But she would not give up trying to communicate with the girl through dreams. Staring out the window at unbroken clouds far below the plane, Major smiled. *In that realm, dear sister, I have power too.*

"Mr. Major," said the pilot's voice over the cabin speaker, "we've started our descent into Toronto."

Soon he would be back in his penthouse apartment, forty stories up in a glass tower on the shore of Lake Ontario. There he would give his servant from the demon world his orders. If the Lady came to the girl in a dream . . . it would be a dream neither would soon forget.

He *would* have that shard back. And in the meantime . . .

Now that the first shard had been found, the second would make its presence known. Next time, he would not underestimate his opponent. And there were two more shards of the blade and then the hilt to be found after that. With each shard he gathered, his power would grow.

He rubbed the ruby stud in his ear. His victory was still certain. Excalibur would be his.

As the pitch of the engine changed and the plane nosed down, he settled back in his seat.

For once, he looked forward to landing.

WALLY SPLUTTERED as chlorine-flavoured water filled his mouth and nose. *Another swimming pool!* He reached for the bottom, but couldn't find it. *And the deep end this time!* Panicking, he floundered . . . but then relaxed when he felt Ariane grab him under the arms and kick for the surface.

They broke through into the air, and he coughed and choked as she swam him to the nearest ladder.

Holding on to it, he looked around. It was dark. The only light came from the red exit signs over the doors, but he recognized the pool. They were in Oscana Collegiate.

Not that he'd spent much time in the school swimming pool, or he wouldn't be drowning every time they arrived somewhere. *Time to sign up for swimming lessons,* he told himself. *First thing tomorrow morning.*

After he'd somehow explained why he'd missed a whole day of classes . . .

They climbed onto the tiled lip and Ariane immediately ordered the water off them. The next instant she sagged against Wally, almost tipping them both into the pool again. He grabbed her shoulders and did his best to keep her upright. "Sorry," she murmured. "So tired . . ."

"Let's get you home," he said.

ALTHOUGH THE SWIMMING pool was closed, the school itself was not. Exhausted almost to the point of fainting, Ariane clung to Wally and tried to look as though they were simply taking an innocent stroll. They received strange looks from the people they passed, and there were far more of them than Ariane expected—or wanted. The school's facilities were frequently rented out to community groups in the evenings, and a number of events seemed to be under-way. In one room they passed, two little girls in kilts pranced around pairs of crossed swords to the taped music of a bagpipe. At the sight of the blades, Ariane put her hand on the pocket where she had placed the first piece of her own sword. Soon enough, Major would know that she had it, if he didn't already. He knew who she was. He knew where she lived.

What would he do next?

As they moved deeper into the school, heading toward the exit on the east side of the building, the one nearest Ariane's house, they left the community groups behind and moved through deserted hallways, past closed, locked classroom doors, their footsteps echoing on the tile floors.

And then, as they entered the final hallway ending in the exit to the school parking lot, the door banged open and they found themselves suddenly face to face with Shania and Felicia and . . . and . . . whatever-the-other-two-girls'-names-were.

The members of the coven weren't wearing school clothes tonight. They were in sweats, and carrying badminton racquets, obviously on their way to the gym. The girls were chattering among themselves, but both the chatter and their forward movement stopped dead when they saw Ariane and Wally. Ariane groaned inwardly. *Great*, she thought. *This is all I need.* She didn't think they'd try to do anything to her in the school, but if they forced her outside, she was too exhausted to draw on the Lady's power to drive them off like last time. *Isn't it bad enough I've got to battle Merlin? Do I have to keep fighting high-school bullies, too?*

"Let us by, Flish," Wally said.

"Shut up." Felicia didn't even look at him. Her eyes were riveted on Ariane. Her face cycled rapidly from white to an unlovely shade of red, verging toward purple. "I owe you." She hefted her badminton racquet as if it were a weapon. "I think we should all go outside and . . . talk." Her friends moved closer. Wally's grip on Ariane's arm tightened.

"I don't want to fight you," Ariane said softly.

Felicia snorted. "I'll bet you don't."

Ariane couldn't stall long enough for her power to regenerate. And without that power, she was helpless. What if they found the shard? If Felicia guessed it was important to Ariane, she would take it, just because she could.

That can't happen! Ariane shoved her hand into her pocket, gripped the shard in her fist . . . and gasped.

Power flooded her—not the Lady's, not her own, but one she didn't recognize, foreign, yet familiar. She felt like a fading flashlight hooked up to a new battery. And more than that, she felt angry. Vengeful. After everything she had been through, these *children* dared to challenge *her*, the Lady of the Lake?

"You don't want to fight *me*, either." Something must have changed in Ariane's voice, because Felicia's eyes widened.

"Says who?" Shania said. She had obviously decided to back up Felicia. She raised her own racquet. She probably meant it to be menacing, but to Ariane, flooded with the power of the shard, she just looked silly as she said, "I'd fight you with one hand tied behind my back."

Enough of this! Ariane smiled. "Will you also fight . . . them?" She exerted a little—*so little!*—of the new energy suffusing her. An ancient trough-like water fountain hung from the wall on her left. All four spouts suddenly turned on. At first the water arced and splashed in the trough—but the arcs grew higher and higher, and then the ends of the arcs pulled free of the drain. Snakelike, the water slipped over the edge of the trough, poured onto the floor, and slithered toward the gang of girls, who stared at them with wide, white eyes.

"It's a trick, just like last time," Felicia yelled. She took a step forward, fist tight around her racquet. "It's just water. It can't hurt you!"

Ariane's smile grew to a teeth-baring grin. "Can't it?" There was something different about this power, something harder and tougher than the Lady's, something that made her want to strike, to break, to bruise, to shatter. The Lady's power could be used that way, but it didn't exult in it. This power *wanted* to be used that way, to be used in *battle* . . .

The soft round ends of the tendrils of water sharpened and hardened into needle-like points of ice. Fast as a striking rattlesnake, one snapped across the corridor, centimetres from Felicia's nose, and hit a locker door with a sound like a rifle shot. It recoiled just as fast, leaving a round hole in the metal.

"Ariane!" Wally cried from behind her. "Stop!"

Ariane heard him, but his plea could not prevail against this new energy filling her. The ice-pointed tendrils rose above the girls, and hovered. "I think you should leave," Ariane said. Her voice trembled. It took all her waning strength to hold back the tendrils. The power wanted to rend and tear, and part of her wanted to let it. "I think you should *run!*"

Felicia's glare didn't waver. But Shania and the other girls had had enough. As one, they turned and dashed away, banging out through the exit and vanishing into the darkness beyond. Felicia looked around, then back at Ariane. "I don't know how you're doing that," she said, "but this isn't over."

She pointed her badminton racquet at Ariane. "You hear me? This isn't over!"

The water-spear inched closer to her. She swatted at it with the racquet, but the mesh simply cut through it without disrupting it at all. Felicia's eyes narrowed. "It's a trick," she said again. "I'll figure it out. And when I do . . ." She backed away, never taking her eyes off Ariane . . . and then she turned and walked, with deliberate casualness, after her friends.

Ariane heaved a deep sigh. The tendrils collapsed, splashing to the floor. With an effort of will, she loosened her aching fingers, releasing the shard of Excalibur. As its power deserted her, she slumped against the lockers. Two boys came around the corner, heading to the exit, and gave them and the puddled water puzzled looks as they passed.

Wally, eyes wide, stared at Ariane as if he'd never seen her before. "You could have killed them," he said. "I thought you were *going* to." He sounded angry, as he had when she had threatened Felicia in the Knights' pool room, but scared as well. "Ariane, she's my sister. You can't . . . please. Don't hurt her."

"It wasn't me." Ariane pulled her shaking hand out of her pocket. "It was the sword. It wants battle. It wants . . . blood." She turned and looked at the hole the water tendril had punched in the metal of the locker. "We have to keep *that* out of Major's hands. We *have* to."

Wally put his finger into the hole. "This isn't going to end well," he muttered.

Ariane didn't reply.

They walked home in silence, going first to Wally's

house. Ariane stopped at the end of the front walk. "What will Felicia do to you?"

"Nothing she doesn't do all the time. Don't worry about me." Wally put his hand on her arm. The gesture almost made her cry. *I must be tired.* "What about you?" Concern warmed his voice. "Will you be all right? Won't Major come after you again?"

"I don't know." But that was a lie. *Yes, he will . . . and after those I love.* And there were other shards out there, somewhere. This one, the sword's point, had been the first. Now that it had been found . . . would she hear the call of the next? She could hear nothing now, with her power drained . . . but her power would return. And if she heard the call of the second shard . . .

. . . she would have to go after it. She'd have no choice. The Lady's power, the power she had willingly—foolishly?— accepted into herself, would insist on it: would not let her rest until she once more followed the song of the sword.

But those were problems for a new day. What she needed now, more than anything else, were food and sleep.

Wally looked as though he were about to say something else, but he seemed to think better of it. Instead he squeezed her arm, then released it. "Good night. Call me tomorrow."

He went inside.

Ariane walked home through a thickening mist. She ran her hand over a parked car as she passed, her fingers skidding over a thin, rough layer of ice. *Winter is coming . . .*

A warm yellow light glowed in the windows of Aunt Phyllis's house. She went inside to find her aunt sitting in her favourite chair in the living room, watching the local news with Pendragon curled up in her lap, the announcer's voice booming, "Police are continuing their investigation into the shocking case of a respected local businessman allegedly caught breaking into the bedroom of a fifteen-year-old girl . . ."

"Hi," Ariane said.

Aunt Phyllis started, then jumped to her feet—much to Pendragon's annoyance—and ran to Ariane, enfolding her in a hug that suddenly, achingly, reminded Ariane of her mother. "I'm so glad you're back. I was getting worried . . ."

"I lost all our camping equipment." It was the first time she'd thought about it.

Aunt Phyllis laughed. "As if that matters!" Her laughter died. "Did you get . . . it?"

Ariane hesitated, then pulled the shard of Excalibur out of her pocket. She felt that greedy surge of aggressive power again—both revolting and . . . attractive. She held up the shard. "Here it is."

Aunt Phyllis looked with wide eyes at the piece of pitted steel. "Oh, my!" She reached out to touch it . . . and then pulled back before her fingers made contact, as though aware of its menacing power. She looked back at Ariane. "But now what?"

Ariane shook her head. "I don't know." She tucked the shard away. "Is there anything to eat?"

WALLY HAD A SURPRISE—HARDLY the first one of the night —when he entered the living room. Instead of Ms. Carson, whom he expected to find sitting ramrod-straight on the couch watching reality TV, and for whom he was already preparing an elaborate story explaining why he'd missed school that day, he saw a portly, balding man with a thick salt-and-pepper beard sitting in the corner armchair, reading the newspaper. A glass of dark beer rested on the table by his right hand. Wally stopped dead. "Dad?" Then he ran to the chair. "Dad!"

His father lowered his newspaper and smiled at him. "Hey, son. Miss me?"

I always do, Wally wanted to say, but something like shyness held him back. His father was so seldom around anymore, it seemed too intimate, like telling a stranger he loved him. He settled for, "Yeah, I guess. Is Mom here too?"

"Ah." His father folded the newspaper with great deliberation, and set it beside his beer. "I think you'd better sit down, Wally. There's something about your mother and me that you need to know . . ."

Ten minutes later Wally was sitting on the frost-covered grass in the back yard, his back pressed against the big tree that had shaded every summer of his life, his knees pulled to his chest. His cheeks were wet from more than the thick, freezing mist. He heard footsteps in the grass, and turned to see Flish, still in her gym clothes, wearing an expression so hard and frozen it wouldn't have looked out of place on an ice sculpture. To his astonishment, she put her back against the tree and slid down into the grass beside him.

"You heard?" he said.

"I heard," Flish said in a voice as cold as the mist. "But I already knew."

"How?" Wally had never guessed. He'd known his parents weren't home much, and that they were travelling separately, but he'd thought it was just work. He'd never dreamed . . .

"Because I live in the real world!" Flish snapped. She glared at him, her eyes glittering hard and sharp as diamond in the light spilling into the yard through the kitchen window. "Because I've been paying attention. I knew about Dad's twenty-something bimbo months ago. In fact, I told Mom about her."

"Months—" That was when Flish had started to change, to become so distant and cold. *"Why didn't you tell me?"*

"Because I figured you'd take Dad's side. You've always been his favourite."

"That's not true!"

"That's what it looks like from here."

Wally didn't want to fight, not now. He looked away, softened his voice. "So what do we do?"

"I've already done it. I'm moving out."

Wally's head snapped around to face her again. "What?"

"I'm old enough. Dad can't keep me here against my will. Shania already lives on her own. I'm moving in with her. Tomorrow."

"But—"

Flish got to her feet. "You're stuck. Too young. Too bad." She put her hands on her hips and stared down at him. "One word of sisterly advice. Stay away from that bitch Ariane. I don't know how she's pulling those tricks, but they won't save her forever. And if you're with her when we take her down . . . well, don't come crying to me." She walked into the house without looking back.

And Walter Arthur Michael Knight the Third, Companion of the Order of the Lady, Sidekick to the Seeker of the Shards, the lucky boy who had found himself on exactly the kind of quest he'd always dreamed about, living the kind of adventure he'd thought only existed in books and video games, put his head down on his knees and bawled like a baby.

ARIANE STOOD AGAIN on the shore of Wascana Lake, staring at that impossible opening in the water. Again she descended the watery stairs and saw the Lady on her throne.

"You have done well," said the Lady. "And now that you have the first shard, I can reach out to you more easily in dreams, to help you as I can. But understand that this is only the beginning. You must find the remaining four pieces of Excalibur: three more shards of the blade, and then the hilt. You must find them before Merlin does. With each piece you possess your power will grow . . . but with each piece he possesses his power will grow. And beware: once all the pieces are found, if Merlin holds the greater part of them, he can call the rest of the sword to him and everything you have tried to achieve will have been in vain."

"I don't like the power I get from Excalibur," Ariane said. "It frightens me."

"It is the power of war. The sword is only happy when it is being wielded in battle. Even when it dwelt with me, I seldom used its power. I feared I would come to love the taste of it too well and seek to rule, as Merlin seeks to rule, instead of to protect. I feared it so much that when I scattered the shards, I even hid them from myself. I cannot tell you where they are. You must listen for them with your power. Listen for the song

of the sword, and shard by shard, Excalibur will be yours. But do not use its power unless you have to. It may destroy more than you wish to be destroyed."

"Did it corrupt Arthur?"

"Arthur was incorruptible, or as near incorruptible as a mortal man may be. No, Excalibur did not corrupt him. It empowered him. He remade his world, and gave birth to a golden age. But he was still human, and that was his undoing. Guinevere betrayed him with his best friend, the kingdom fell into civil war, and his bastard son Mordred fought against him. Both fell and Excalibur returned to me. I broke it and scattered it. The golden age of Camelot fell into chaos and bloodshed. A dark age descended. But not as dark as the age which awaits your world if Merlin re-forges the sword."

"She liesss," a new voice said from behind Ariane, a voice as soft as silk and as sibilant as a snake's hiss. If she turned around, she would see the speaker, but so horrifying was the voice, she feared coming face-to-face with its owner. "Liesss . . . my massster bringsss order in place of chaossss . . . he will thrust thisss world to greatnesss and remake hisss own . . . give him the shard . . . help him find the othersss . . . he will reward you well . . ."

"How came you here?" the Lady thundered. "This is not your world! Begone!"

"I think not." The voice held a hint of a cold chuckle. "Thisss is not your world either, Lady. And the door isss almossst closed. Your power is ssstretched too thin for you to command me. Though my massster's power hasss waned with the agesss, he dwellsss in thisss world, on thisss ssside of the door to Faerie. It isss you who mussst begone, Lady. For now, and for alwaysss!"

A flare of red light like that of a bonfire, a hiss like water falling on hot coals, and the Lady cried out and vanished in a thick cloud of steam that erupted all around Ariane, wrapping her in dim greyness.

She turned and turned and turned again, seeking an exit. She saw a dim glow and stepped toward it, but as she did so it resolved into two red gleams, side by side.

Eyes!

"I cannot touch you, Lady," said . . . whatever it was. "You know thisss . . . the sssword, until my massster takesss it from you, protectsss you . . .

But know thisss, too, Lady. My massster will take it from you . . . sssoon. And when he doesss . . . I will be here, in your dreamsss . . . and you will be mine!"

ARIANE WOKE SUDDENLY, with no transition at all. She stared at the dark ceiling of her room, her heart pounding.

She rolled over and looked at the shard, lying on the table beside her bed.

Do not use it unless you have to, the Lady had said in her dream.

But she had also said, *It is a thing of war* . . . and like it or not, she was *in* a war, a war between ancient powers who had somehow reached forward through centuries and across whole worlds to ensnare her in their conflict.

Her half-night's sleep had replenished her powers. Deep inside, she could hear a distant song, faint, diffuse, impossible to pinpoint yet, but definitely there—the song of the second piece of Arthur's legendary sword.

She had won a battle, but the war . . .

. . . the war was just beginning.

She put the first shard of Excalibur under her pillow, stared into the darkness, and waited for the morning.

THE END

DON'T MISS THE REST OF THE
SHARDS OF EXCALIBUR SERIES

WWW.SHARDSOFEXCALIBUR.COM

Twist of the Blade
Aurora Award finalist for
Best Young Adult Novel

"A satisfying second instalment . . . Twist of the Blade offers an enticing sense of danger and excitement as Ariane pursues her mission, but the narrative doesn't shy away from the story's human elements . . . It's refreshing to read a story in which the heroes and villains are not cut-and-dried, and readers can look forward to three more instalments in this genuinely entertaining myth-based series."
– Quill & Quire

Lake in the Clouds

"Well written and fast-moving, with touches of humour, Lake in the Clouds will appeal to young readers who enjoy adventure as well as adults who might like a modern visit to the timeless story of King Arthur and his knights. Recommended."
– Ronald Hore, CM Magazine

Cave Beneath the Sea

*"In Cave Beneath the Sea, Edward Willett has created as
exciting a read as the earlier books in the series, continuing to
develop his characters and their relationships while the
action-filled plot carries the reader to intriguing national and
international locales . . ."*
– Helen Kubiw, *CanLit for Little Canadians*

Door into Faerie
**Aurora Award finalist
for Best Young Adult Novel**

*"I loved this YA fantasy. Willett wields his well-honed writing
chops from page one, and my interest was maintained until
the final word"I can't imagine teens not enjoying this
entertaining story, perhaps especially if they've read the books
that've preceded it. This adult enjoyed it, too . . ."*
– Shelley A. Leedahl, *SaskBooks Reviews*

***Available as Audiobooks on Audible
Narrated by Elizabeth Klett***

ABOUT THE AUTHOR

EDWARD WILLETT is the author of more than sixty books of science fiction, fantasy, and nonfiction for readers of all ages, including twelve novels for DAW Books, most recently the humorous outer-space adventure *The Tangled Stars*. *Marseguro* (DAW Books) won the Aurora Award (honouring Canadian science fiction and fantasy) for Best Long-Form Work in English and his young adult fantasy *Spirit Singer* (also available from Shadowpaw Press) won a Saskatchewan Book Award for best book by a Regina author.

Several other of his books have been shortlisted for those and other awards, including *Star Song*, his most recent novel for Shadowpaw Press, which was shortlisted for the Aurora Award for Best Young Adult Novel.

His nonfiction runs the gamut from science books to biographies to history, and he hosts the Aurora Award-winning podcast *The Worldshapers*, in which he talks to other science fiction and fantasy authors about their creative process. A former newspaper reporter and editor, Ed is also a professional actor and singer. He lives in Regina, Saskatchewan, with his wife, Margaret Anne Hodges, P.Eng., a past president of the Association of Professional Engineers and Geoscientists of Saskatchewan. They have one daughter and a much younger black Siberian cat, after whom Shadowpaw Press is named.

You can find Ed online at www.edwardwillett.com.

 facebook.com/edward.willett

 twitter.com/ewillett

 instagram.com/edwardwillettauthor

ALSO FROM SHADOWPAW PRESS

Thickwood

By Gayle M. Smith

The Emir's Falcon

By Matt Hughes

One Lucky Devil

The First World War Memoirs of Sampson J. Goodfellow

By Sampson J. Goodfellow

Paths to the Stars

Twenty-Two Fantastical Tales of Imagination

By Edward Willett

Shapers of Worlds

Shapers of Worlds Volume II

Shapers of Worlds Volume III

Science fiction and fantasy by authors who were guests on the award-winning podcast *The Worldshapers*

Star Song

By Edward Willett

New editions of notable, previously published books

Stay

By Katherine Lawrence

Duatero

By Brad C. Anderson

Blue Fire

By E.C. Blake

Phases

By Belinda Betker

Legend of Sarah

Cat's Pawn

Cat's Gambit

Cat's Game

By Leslie Gadallah

The Crow Who Tampered With Time

Backwater Mystic Blues

By Lloyd Ratzlaff

The Shards of Excalibur Series

The Peregrine Rising Duology

Spirit Singer

From the Street to the Stars

By Edward Willett

Dollybird

By Anne Lazurko

Small Reckonings

By Karin Melberg Schwier

The Ghosts of Spiritwood

By Martine Noël-Maw

www.ingramcontent.com/pod-product-compliance
Lightning Source LLC
Chambersburg PA
CBHW070452200726

48293CB00007B/2174